His image was clearer now. A s  *shaded lamp in the living room like a spotlight to reveal his slumped form. His head jerked. He cocked it to the right, listening to something Katie could not hear. Then he looked toward the house.*

Katie looked too. She saw nothing but shadows. Dark, sinister shadows. She tried to suppress a shudder, but failed, gasping instead as one of the shadows detached itself from the others. It grew thicker, and almost imperceptibly, it began to move toward the railing. Katie looked to see the boy slumped over the railing. She called out to him but he did not, or he could not hear. It didn't matter which. The result was the same. The shadow grew, taking on human form, and moved closer to the boy who appeared to be asleep, with his head pillowed on the cracked railing. Katie tried again to call out a warning. Her voice disappeared like dust in the wind. She tried to move forward to warn him; her feet sank into the soft wood of the deck, and she was unable to move. She watched in absolute terror as the shadow advanced on the unsuspecting boy and pushed.

L.M. Henderson

Final Justice

For my sister Jean
love Lynn.

PINE LAKE BOOKS

West Guilford

ISBN: 978-0-9813539-3-7

Pine Lake Books

West Guilford, Ontario
pinelakebooks@gmail.com
www.pinelakebooks.webs.com

For the Rugrats

Prologue

HER CARROT RED hair was in piglets, and her dark freckles stood out on her pale face. She beckoned Katie to follow her into the woods.

Katie shook her head. She wasn't supposed to go into the woods. It wasn't safe in the woods. There were wild animals, maybe wolves, besides she might get lost. Katie was definitely not going in the woods.

The little redheaded girl beckoned Katie to follow, but Katie stubbornly refused. The woods were dark, and scary. She was not going into the woods. The words were a mantra in her brain, but her legs had a will of their own, and they carried her into the woods.

The sun didn't quite make it through the heavy canopy of the trees, and Katie shivered. She didn't want to be here. More than anything else in the world, she wanted to be back at the cottage with her mom, and Luke, but something compelled her to follow the strange little girl.

Deeper into the woods they went, until Katie was sure she would never find her way out. Suddenly, the little girl stopped and pointed to a spot on the ground. The ground looked different here. There weren't as many leaves, or pine needles. The ground beneath this tree was almost bare.

Katie dropped to her knees, and started clawing at the earth with her bare hands. The ground was harder than it looked, and her fingernails broke. The ends of her fingers began to bleed, and still Katie dug. Her fingers hit something hard and smooth, and she was suddenly terrified. Icy fear twisted around her heart, and her heart beat erratically. It was getting hard to breath. She didn't want to dig anymore. She glanced up to see the girl sitting on the ground with her arms wrapped around her legs. She was rocking back and forth, and staring at the hole in the ground. "Don't stop, Katie," she whispered. Her voice reflected the fear Katie felt. "Don't leave me here." Slowly Katie cleared the dirt away, and found herself staring into the dead eyes of the stranger.

Katie screamed.

One

HIS IMAGE WAS clearer now. A stream of light from a single, shaded lamp in the living room behind crept across the deck like a spotlight to reveal his slumped form. His head jerked. He cocked it to the right, listening to something Katie could not hear. Then he looked toward the house.

Katie looked too. She saw nothing but shadows. Dark, sinister shadows. She tried to suppress a shudder, but failed, gasping instead as one of the shadows detached itself from the others. It grew thicker, and almost imperceptibly, it began to move toward the railing. Katie looked to see the boy slumped over the railing. She called out to him but he did not, or he could not hear. It didn't matter which. The result was the same.

The shadow grew, taking on human form, and moved closer to the boy who appeared to be asleep, with his head pillowed on the cracked railing. Katie tried again to call out a warning. Her voice disappeared like dust in the wind. She tried to move forward to warn him; her feet sank into the soft wood of the deck, and she was unable to move. She watched in absolute terror as the shadow advanced on the unsuspecting boy and pushed.

His eyes widened in surprise. Katie could tell they were intelligent eyes clear now of any of the earlier fogginess. Surprise turned to recognition, then disbelief, and finally shock as the railing he was leaning on gave way.

Katie moved then. She reached the railing in time to see the hapless boy, arms and legs flailing, drift almost in slow motion through the trees to the ground below. The sickening thud as his body hit the pine carpeted woods below belied the speed with which he fell.

Katie stared at the broken body below her. His arms were akimbo, one leg bent almost completely behind his back, his neck twisted like a ragdoll. There was no way the boy had survived the fall. Katie turned from the horrid sight, her mouth covered to prevent the rising bile from spewing forth. However, when she turned it was not vomit that spewed forth, but a scream. One long, terrified eruption as the shadow moved again.

Toward Katie.

She sat straight up, and let the air rushing in the open car window blow away the remnant cobwebs of the dream. Already the images were gone. Only the terror and a feeling of utter helplessness remained.

"Jeesh, Katie," complained Matt. "You nearly made me pee my pants. Why'd you scream like that?"

Katie glared at her little half brother, only to catch the flickering of the movie Matt was watching. A shadow was moving stealthily behind a teenage boy, who of course was completely oblivious to his immediate danger, just as he'd been the first two times the movie was on today. Katie rolled her eyes. "Don't you ever get tired of watching that garbage," she said. No wonder she was having nightmares. Matt was a complete horror movie junkie, and 'The Shadow' was his favorite.

"It's not garbage." Matt's voice was sulky. He couldn't understand why Katie didn't share his love of horror. "These are classics. They don't make movies like these anymore."

"Of course not," Katie said. "Nowadays movies are in color."

Her mother twisted in her seat, her worried eyes scanning Katie's face even as she scolded. "Don't tease your brother, Katie. At least the movies are keeping him occupied."

"I'm sorry," Katie said. With an exaggerated sigh, she turned back to look out the window.

Katie watched as town after little town flew by. Picturesque places with quaint little names like Glenarm, Woodville, and Coboconk. She was tired, and her legs were beginning to cramp. Six hours in a car was too long, she decided. She didn't even have the energy to tease Matt any more.

Two

"LUKE, SLOW DOWN. We don't want to drive past the place."

Katie grinned at her mother's words. She was always telling Luke to slow down. You would think he was in the habit of getting lost—which was definitely not true. Katie couldn't remember a single time her stepfather had gotten lost. He had a sixth sense for direction, and he proved it again now by slowing down, and signaling before Irene saw the sign she was watching for.

He turned left off the highway, and followed the curve to the left. "Weren't you supposed to turn right?" her mother asked, looking at the map on her lap.

"Not until after the bridge," replied Luke.

There was a sign on the side of a garage that said there was a wolf center a few kilometers away. Katie hoped that would be something Bill would like to see. They crossed a small concrete bridge, rounded the end of the lake, and then turned at the next right. They drove down the dirt road for a couple of minutes. The lake was close to the right hand side of the road, and all the houses were on the left. The houses were few, and set on large lots. Some were small, no more than cottages, others were low and rambling, like ranch houses. Katie spotted a couple of horses in a field behind one of the houses, and even a few cows. They definitely weren't in the city anymore.

Katie held her breath as they drove past a small graveyard, and a tiny white church. There were several old people wandering around the tombstones, and a little girl was picking wild flowers near the edge of the woods. An old man stared straight at her. His black vacant eyes were red rimmed.

"Help me," he mouthed. Katie couldn't hear him, but it didn't matter. She couldn't help him with anything. He was already dead.

"Ha," Luke exclaimed as he turned into the entrance of the camp grounds. "Right where I thought it would be." Everyone laughed when Irene hit him with the map she was holding. "Hey, don't wreck the map," Luke teased. "We wouldn't want to get lost before we get to Algonquin."

"No way," piped Matt. At six Matt was never sure when his parents were serious, and when they were teasing. "I want to see the deer." From the moment Luke had mentioned a vacation in Algonquin Park, Matt had talked of nothing else. The only thing better than deer that were not afraid of people—deer that came right up to you and ate out of the palm of your hand—were reindeer.

There was a fork in the road, and Luke chose the road to the right. Of course, it led to a large, A-frame building. A sign on a hook flipped to `Open', hung just below a more permanent sign that said `Office'.

"This is it." Luke pulled into a parking spot in front of the office, and turned off the engine. "Let's find out where you're staying."

While Irene and Matt waited in the van, much to Matt's annoyance, Katie and Luke went into the building. It wasn't much of an office. Luke spoke to a short, slightly plump woman with a friendly expression.

"Hi," he said. "I'm Luke Williams, and this is my daughter, Katie. We are looking for Bill Davis."

"Maggie," the woman said, as she pulled out a book from under the counter where a couple men sat drinking coffee. "Let's see, Davis. Aw, here it is. Bill Davis. He has the Outlook for a month."

Katie listened with one ear, while she took in her surroundings. Along one wall were a couple of shelves with candy, bread, and potato chips. A cooler holding milk and pop stood in a corner beside a door leading to a dining room. Through that door, she saw six tables, four of them occupied. Through the door to her left, Katie saw a bar with eight stools, and three more tables. There was a giant television over the bar, and a dartboard on the wall at the end.

"Thanks," Matt said, drawing Katie's attention back to the conversation. "Got it," he winked at Katie.

"I thought you were getting directions to the cabin, Luke?" asked Irene, when they returned to the car waving the key on the end of a stick.

"I did," replied Luke.

"Well it looks strangely like a key to me. What does it do, beep when we get close?"

Katie laughed, when Matt asked, "Does it really beep?" For such a smart little boy, he really did ask some stupid questions.

"Where's Bill?" asked Irene, her voice tense. "Did he even bother to show up?"

Luke put his hand on his wife's shoulder. "Calm down, Reno," he murmured. Reno was his pet name for Irene, although Katie never understood where it came from. Probably something to do with them meeting in Reno. "Bill hasn't arrived yet."

"What do you mean, Bill hasn't arrived yet?" Luke may have spoken calmly, but Katie had no trouble detecting the growing anger in Irene's voice.

Great! Perfect way to start a holiday. Mom pissed at Bill, Katie thought. *It would be just like her to change her mind about me staying for the month.*

"Just what I said." Luke spoke soothingly as if he were talking to an irate child. "Bill is running a little late. He could arrive at any moment. Mrs. Mitchell, that's the woman in the office," Luke explained. "Mrs. Mitchell said Bill made all the arrangements by mail. But he phoned last week to verify everything, and paid in full." Katie couldn't miss the telltale pink splashes on her mother's cheeks. She was angry, but before Irene could say anything Luke continued. "Maybe his plane was late, or there was a problem at customs. Whatever the reason, I'm sure he'll be here just as soon as he can."

The road wound from the office, past several trailers, and then up a steep hill into the forest. They drove by several cabins, each in their own secluded spot, before Luke stopped the van in front of the last cabin at the end of the road. The sign above the door of the cabin read `Outlook`. "Come on," Luke said, as always his was the calmer voice. "Let's get Katie's things inside. We still have a few hours driving, and I'd like to make Algonquin before dark." He tossed Katie the key.

Katie pushed open the door, and her breath caught in her throat. The open concept made the cabin seem much larger on the inside than it was on the outside. The sun shining through the patio door made the hardwood floor gleam. The kitchen was to the right. There were cupboards, counters, fridge, stove, and a small table set so you could look out the patio door. To her left there were three open doors, two obviously bedrooms, and the middle one the bathroom. The rest of the cabin was living room.

"Get moving, Katie." Luke gave her a nudge, and she stumbled into the room. "If you aren't going to help at least move so we can bring your stuff in."

"Sorry, Dad." Katie ran back to the van to help with the rest of her luggage.

The cabin was larger than Katie expected. The open area, including the kitchen area, was large enough to hold at least a dozen people. The only rug in the room was a small area rug in front of the real fireplace. Katie couldn't help thinking that a bearskin rug would not have been out of place, but even without one, she loved the stone fireplace. There was a pile of logs in the wood crib, and Katie had no problem picturing a crackling fire. There were two couches, both looked like the kind that converted into beds, she had a similar one back home, and several overstuffed chairs.

A shadow by the patio doors caught Katie's attention. She dropped her bag on the floor by the bedroom door, and went out on the deck. She caught a glimpse of the lake in the distance. Sunbeams bounced off the surface like jewels. A teenage boy, wearing dirty blue jeans, and a red t-shirt was leaning nonchalantly on the railing. Katie could see him as clearly as she could see the lake, and the trees through him. Residual or ghost, she wondered.

There was a time when Katie didn't know there was a difference between a residual haunting, and a ghost, much less what that difference was. That was a long time ago, and a lot had changed since then. Since then, Katie had learned to deal with her *gift*, and by deal with, she meant for the most part, ignore.

Katie cleared her throat, and the boy disappeared. She closed her eyes, and opened them again very slowly. Still gone. Good. He was gone, and it was not happening again. Katie was on vacation, and intended to enjoy herself, not deal with the problems of dead people. She took a deep breath, and forced all thoughts of the boy from her mind.

The cabin was on the side of a steep hill, surrounded by forest. Each cabin was on its own secluded lot, offering the privacy that Bill desired. Katie would have preferred a trailer closer to the others, but she understood Bill's need for solitude. He may be spending the month with her, but he would be working. There was no doubt in her mind.

Katie walked across the stained deck that wrapped around three sides of the cabin, and leaned on the railing that was so new it looked out of place with the aged wood of the deck. She peered down at the carpet of pine needles below. A knot formed in the pit of her stomach, and she swallowed convulsively. For a moment, a heartbeat only, she could see the body of a teenage boy wearing blue jeans and a red t-shirt, sprawled awkwardly on the ground below. The boy she'd seen leaning against the old railing. It was only a flicker, but she felt the cold tentacles of fear clutching her throat. Even here, she was not going to be free from them. She nearly screamed when a hand clasped her shoulder.

"Katie?" Luke asked his concern evident in his eyes. "Are you okay? I called you three times."

Katie blinked, and the scene was gone. There was nothing below except for the forest floor, covered with a bed of pine needles. If only it would stay that way. "I'm fine, Dad." Katie had to force her voice to sound normal. It wasn't always easy hiding her visions from those closest to her.

"I was just thinking how nice it's going to be to swim in the lake," she forced a cheerfulness she didn't feel into her voice. "This place is great. I'm going to have a blast here." She linked her arm through Luke's, and together they went into the cabin to find Irene and Matt.

Irene was in the smaller of the two bedrooms, Katie's suitcase opened on the bed. The walls were a pale green, and the floor was polished wood. A small window looked onto the woods behind the cabin. There was a chest with three drawers under the window, and a small armoire beside it. There was no closet in the room. On the other side of the window was a small writing desk and chair. There was a small clock/radio sitting on the desk. At the bottom of the bed was a captain's bench, and in the corner was another of those overstuffed chairs, with a reading lamp behind it.

"Let me do that, Mom," Katie said. She took the sweater her mother was holding, and shoved it back into the suitcase. "It will give me something to do while I wait for Bill."

Luke looked at his watch. "It's almost three now. Why don't we grab a bite to eat? By that time Bill should be here. If not, then I'm sure Katie will be fine until he does get here. He can't be that much longer."

They all climbed into the van, and drove down the hill to the restaurant. The place was small, and cozy. A couple of men sat at the counter drinking coffee, and talking. Other than that, they were the only ones in the restaurant. They chose a table near the window where they could glimpse the lake through the trees. Mrs. Mitchell took their order, cooked the food, and served them herself. "It's pretty quiet right now," she told them. "I usually have a girl that helps me, but she doesn't come in until the supper rush."

Less than an hour later, Katie stood outside the restaurant and waved goodbye to her family. It had been touch and go for a while, Irene wasn't sure she wanted to leave Katie alone. Bill had never been the most reliable person when it came to his personal life. Katie remembered several times when she and her mom had waited for Bill, and he had not shown up, or else he had shown up days later. To add insult to injury, he wouldn't call to say he was going to be late, or that he wasn't coming. That was one of the reasons Irene had finally divorced Bill. He was unreliable—but only in his personal life. He was very reliable when it came to his job as a foreign correspondent. He had to be.

After the divorce, Irene met Luke, and before she knew it she was head over heels, and agreeing to marry him. Luke was Bill's complete opposite, a real family man. He spent as much time as possible with them. Picnics, camping trips, ball games. It didn't matter what they did as long as they were together. Best of all, when Luke said he'd be some place, he was, and on time. He treated Katie like his own daughter, had from the very beginning, and it wasn't long before she was calling him Dad.

Bill didn't seem to mind. He actually seemed happy that Katie had Luke for a dad. That left him free to come and go as he pleased, without the guilt. It was only in the past four years that Katie and Bill had developed a good relationship. Probably because I can take care of myself, thought Katie.

Whatever the reason, Katie was looking forward to spending the month with him.

Katie was still looking down the road in the direction her family had gone when the door behind her opened. Mrs. Mitchell saw her, and hurried over. She was a friendly, plump woman with mousy brown hair cut in a bob just below her ears.

"Oh good," she said. "You're still here." She looked around the parking lot, and frowned. "Has your mother left already?"

"Only just, Mrs. Mitchell," Katie answered. "Is there something you needed?"

"Oh, call me Maggie. Everyone does." A couple of kids ran past them into the store. "Slow down you two," Mrs. Mitchell scolded. "I don't allow running in my place." The kids dutifully slow their pace to a fast walk, giggling as they went. "Now what was I saying? Oh, yes. Mr. Davis is on the phone asking to speak to your mother. I guess you will do. Come with me."

Katie followed the short woman into the office, and waited until she left before picking up the receiver. "Hello," she ventured. "Bill?"

"Katie? It's good to hear your voice. Is your mother there?"

"Not exactly."

"What do you mean, not exactly? Either she's there or she's not."

"They just left," Katie admitted. "Where are you?"

"I'm at the airport" he hedged.

That wasn't too bad. He could be here in three hours, more or less. Katie was a lot like her father, and she notice the wary note in his voice. What was he not saying, and how was it going to affect her? "In Toronto, right?" she asked, hesitantly, her fingers crossed. *Please don't let me down this time.*

"Actually, I'm in Scotland. I tried to call before I left, but I missed you."

Great, thought Katie. *The first time mom lets me spend time alone with him, and he doesn't bother to show up.* Then she felt guilty. She hadn't even asked why he was in Scotland when he was supposed to be in London, but she would lay odds it was for work. Whenever Bill got a lead, large or small, all thoughts of his family flew out of his head. "What are you doing in Scotland, Bill?" Katie had not called him Dad in a very long time. He might be her father, but Luke was more of a dad.

"I was all ready to leave, when I got a hot tip on a man I've been trying to track down for several weeks now.

26

According to my source, he is in Edinburgh. Listen, Katie. I am sorry about not being there, but this could be my only chance of finding this person. You do understand, don't you?" Of course, she understood. What did spending time with his daughter mean, compared to his precious job.

It should not have come as a surprise. It wasn't the first time her father had failed to show. You would think she would be used to it by now, but although she wouldn't admit it to anybody, it hurt—a lot. He didn't know that she spent weeks trying to convince her mother that he had changed. That he would not stand her up again, even though she didn't have any proof. Sure, he had shown up the last three times when he said he would, give or take an hour. Then, again, he had only visited her three times in the past two years, and those times conveniently coincided with assignments stateside. "Sure, Dad, I understand." She tried to hide the disappointment she was feeling, without success. "I'll call the ranger station at Algonquin, and leave a message for Luke to come back and get me."

"You know, Katie. I was thinking. I shouldn't be any more than a day or two at the most. The plane is ready to go, and the pilot is on standby. I'll be there as soon as possible. I'm really looking forward to spending time together. Do you think you would be okay alone for a couple of days? If not, you could go with your mother and I will pick you up there as soon as I can. You're old enough to stay alone for a couple days, aren't you?"

Katie mentally rolled her eyes. Didn't the man have any idea how old she was? As far as she was concerned, she was plenty old enough to stay alone. She had to think about it for less than a moment. Let's see, a day or two alone, no kid brother pestering her, no well-meaning parents telling her what to do, and when to do it. She had her own money from her part time job, so she wasn't going to starve. "I can't see a single reason why I wouldn't be okay alone," she finally said when she realized Bill was waiting for an answer. "I'll see you in a day or two."

Three

KATIE DECIDED TO explore the campgrounds, and see who her neighbors were. She thought fleetingly of calling her mother to let her know what had happened. She did have the number for the rangers' office at Algonquin, in case of emergencies. But, was this an emergency. Irene would see it that way, but Katie was afraid that if Luke had to come get her now, her mom wouldn't let her come with Bill when he did show up. She decided against calling. It would take Luke at least three hours to get to the park, and another three hours to get back here, and then another three to get there again. That was a lot of driving, and Katie had no doubt he *would* come and get her. Irene would insist on it. She justified her decision by convincing herself that Bill could possibly be there by tomorrow, and then Luke would have spent all that time driving for nothing, when he should have been with Irene and Matt.

Outside the office, there was a signpost with several arrows pointing in different directions. The one pointing down the road that led to the entrance and the lake, obviously said `LAKE'. The arrow pointing to the road that led to the cabin, said `CABINS', and another arrow pointed to a road that was no more than a wide dirt path. This sign said `TENTS'. Katie could see several tents in the large field, and the smoke from a couple of campfires hovered in the still air. Someone must have been cooking, because it was too hot just to have a fire.

She strolled slowly down the lake road, until she came to the playground. Several maple trees spread around the campground, providing much needed shade on hot days.

Between the trailers were cedar hedges, offering privacy to the occupants. Katie stopped to watch two little girls about three years old playing on a teeter-totter, when she heard her name called.

"Katie. Hello, Katie." A girl about Katie's height, with long brown hair was hurrying along the road in her direction, and waving her hands frantically. "Wait there, Katie," she called.

Finally, out of breath, the girl stood in front of Katie. Her eyes were so pale they reminded Katie of an actor she liked who was always playing blind people. The girl's smile was friendly, and Katie thought instantly of Mrs. Mitchell.

"Hi. I'm Daina. Daina Mitchell. Mom sent me to find you. You forgot this." Daina dangled a key from a small piece of wood with the word OUTLOOK painted on it in front of Katie. "In the office," she continued, needlessly indicating the direction she had just come from with a jerk of her head.

Katie felt stupid. She must have set the key down when she was talking to Bill on the phone. What a great way to prove she could look after herself, losing her key the moment she was alone. Something of what she was thinking must have shown on her face because Daina laughed.

"Don't sweat it," she told Katie. "Most people don't worry about keys around here. They just unlock their cabin,

31

and then leave the key inside until they leave." She handed Katie the key. "Mom only locks them when they're empty so kids can't party in them. She thinks that's all teenagers do is party."

"Well, thanks for bringing it to me." Katie accepted the key with a question. "Did you have any trouble finding me?"

"You're a stranger. Strangers stand out around here." Daina shrugged. "That, and mom saw you heading this way, and pointed you out to me."

"Let's hope I don't stay a stranger for too long." Katie laughed nervously. "I don't have ten or twenty years to become a local."

Daina laughed with her. "Well you're not a stranger to me anymore."

"Gee," Katie tilted her head, and looked at Daina contemplatively. "Now that I'm not a stranger, maybe you can show me where everyone hangs out." In for a penny, in for a pound her mom always said. If she wanted to make friends while she was here this summer, she may as well start now.

Daina didn't answer immediately, and Katie was afraid she didn't want to introduce her around. Then Daina grinned. "Sure, no problem. You would have found them soon enough anyway if you stayed on the lake road. There's usually a volleyball game around this time."

They continued along the lake road, passing several trailers before rounding a bend, and coming upon a group of children playing ring-a-ring of posies in front of a small trailer with a large add-a-room.

Katie paused to watch them. She didn't notice the small beagle sleeping on the deck, until she saw a blur, and heard it barking. Katie couldn't stop the quick scream that rose in her throat. She closed her eyes, and her hands clenched into small fists at her sides. She waited for the inevitable pain. It never occurred to her to run. Her heart beat frantically as memories flooded her mind.

They were playing monkey in the middle—Katie, with her cousins Frank and Lisa. Frank, who was almost two years older than Katie, was in the middle. Lisa threw the ball ... High ... It sailed over Frank's head. It sailed over Katie's head. Katie laughed at the astounded look on Frank's face. Who would have thought that Lisa could throw so far? She turned to watch the ball. It landed on the crest of a knoll, paused for a minute, and then it rolled down the other side.

Katie followed the ball over the knoll, and down the other side. She followed the ball into the long grass at the edge of the park. It was while she was kicking over the long grass

*looking for the elusive ball that she came upon the stray. It had
dirty black fur, matted with blood. It was crouched over what
looked suspiciously like the broken, bloody body of a cat.*

*Katie could not stop the scream that rose in her throat.
The stray turned black, hate-filled eyes toward the frightened
intruder. Katie ran. The dog chased her. Katie got about ten
steps when the stray pounced. She screamed once more as she
collapsed like a rag doll. The pain in her left leg was
excruciating. There was blood everywhere. Somebody else was
screaming so loud now it hurt Katie's ears. Unable to endure
any more she closed her eyes, and allowed the darkness to
embrace her in its comforting arms.*

Although the physical pain was gone, the scars on her
psyche were a long way from healed.

"Katie? Katie? What's wrong? What happened?"

The voice reached Katie through the fog. She felt
comfort in the hands that gripped her shoulders enough to be
painful. She opened her eyes and for a split second, she
thought she glimpsed glee in the face before her, and then the
worry on Daina's face made her ashamed. The children, only
moments before laughing and playing, looked at her with a
mixture of curiosity and fear. The small beagle lay curled up at

the end of his rope—still on the deck, satisfied that she posed no threat to the children.

"I'm sorry," she stuttered. "I thought ... the dog. Never mind what I thought," she finally said, pulling herself together. "Let's go to the lake." Katie tried to ignore the burning in her left calf, as she limped along the lake road.

A small stand of pine trees separated the beach from the volleyball net. About a dozen kids were already playing.

"Hi, guys." Daina waved to the small group. "This is Katie. She arrived today."

"Hey, Katie," they answered in unison, before turning back to the game.

Daina and Katie sat on the sidelines. They chose opposite sides to cheer. Katie's side won. There was plenty of good natured ribbing between the opposing teams, as well as a great deal of back slapping with "way to go," among the winners, and "we'll get them next time," among the losers. *Everybody knows everybody*, thought Katie. They seem such good friends, that Katie was trying to imagine what it would be like to belong. She was deep into her daydreaming, and didn't notice anyone approach.

"Earth to Katie. Earth to Katie. Come in, Katie." A redheaded boy with freckles plopped himself on the grass beside Katie. "You do talk, don't you?"

Katie blushed. Then she laughed nervously. "Of course I talk," she finally spit out. Her mom was always telling her not to be so shy. Get out there and meet people, she was always saying. Easy for her mom. She was beautiful, and everyone loved her. Katie, on the other hand, was shy, insecure, and cursed with the ability to see ghosts. Maybe if she could keep her strange ability from becoming public knowledge she could make some friends this summer.

Red, as Katie was already thinking of him, pulled a handful of grass and threw it at Katie. It missed and hit Daina. Katie laughed before she could stop herself. Daina jumped up and frantically began clawing at the grass in her hair. She glared at Red and Katie. "I'll get you for this," she threatened in a low voice. Katie shuddered. It was not the words, but rather the hatred she glimpsed in Daina's blue eyes that caused her reaction. The next instant Daina was smiling, making Katie doubt herself. "Hey, guys," she said more loudly. "Let's go for a swim."

Daina ignored Katie all the time they were playing in the water. Katie tried talking to her when they were standing on the dock, but Daina jumped into the water without acknowledging her. Later Katie saw her talking to a couple of other girls. Katie got a sinking feeling in the pit of her stomach when the group looked toward her, and then turned away quickly.

A tall boy with long, brown hair pushed Katie into the water, and all thoughts of Daina vanished as the cold water closed over her head.

Back on the beach, the dark haired boy, she though his name was Pete, offered Katie his towel. "Thank you," Katie said. She wiped the water from her face and hands, and handed it back. "I wasn't really planning on swimming," she told him. "I haven't even unpacked yet." *Great*, Katie thought. *I'm babbling. The poor guy is only trying to be nice. He doesn't care whether I've unpacked.* Katie watched warily, as Daina and her friends came out of the water. They kept sneaking looks her way, and every time Katie looked back they quickly averted their eyes.

Soon there was a small crowd on the beach. Katie couldn't help noticing that the girls all seemed to be keeping their distance. Even some of the boys had started looking at her strangely. Maybe this place wasn't going to be so different after all.

"Where's the party tonight, folks?" Red broke her reverie with his question. "Can't have it at my place. Mom's still mad about her garden. Yuck. What a mess." Everyone laughed. "So, where's it going to be?"

Here's my chance, Katie thought. *I can align myself with these people now. Or I can spend the rest of the summer on the outside looking in. Besides, I have the cabin to myself.* She took a deep, fortifying breath, and before she could change her mind, she blurted. "You can party at my place."

"Won't your parents mind?" asked Pete, his head tilted slightly as he watched her expression.

Maybe this wasn't such a good idea, but she couldn't back out now. "No. Actually, I have the place to myself tonight."

"Sounds great," said Red. "Where are you?"

"She's in the Outlook," said Daina, bitterness loud in her voice. She had a smug look on her face.

Katie watched in confusion, as towels and belongings were gathered, and everyone left. One moment, everybody seemed to be talking at once, yet nobody actually said anything to Katie, the next she was standing on the empty beach.

Four

KATIE LAY ON the deck staring at the Milky Way. There must be a zillion or so stars twinkling above. She had never seen this many stars in the sky above their house in New York. They might be there, somewhere above the smog and the city lights, but she'd never seen them. She listened to the wind whispering through the leaves, and the song of a nearby cricket. The scent of pine tickled her nose.

She could hardly credit that she was here alone, and not the least bit scared. It had taken her nearly fifteen minutes to follow the road to the Outlook. She passed the other cabins, but couldn't tell if they were empty. Most of the road was uphill through the woods. *Over the hill and through the woods to grandma's house I go.* Katie felt a little like Little Red Riding Hood. It was just her, the birds and the squirrels. More than once, she felt eyes on her, watching her. She kept waiting for the big bad wolf to jump out from the security of the surrounding woods, but he never showed.

Soon she heard something over the gentle rustling of the leaves. Buzz. She sat perfectly still, barely breathing. She hoped the mosquito would decide she wouldn't make a very good dinner. Soon she began to hear other sounds in the woods. The chirping cricket accompanied by the kerr-ump, kerr-ump of a bullfrog. A twig snapped as some creature of the night stalked its dinner.

Katie watched the stars, and listened to the music of the night. She still wasn't sure what had happened at the lake, but she was certain nobody was coming to the cabin tonight. Nobody showed up while she finished unpacking. Nobody came while she was trying to light a fire in the outside pit. Now that was a disaster. An entire newspaper later, and all she managed to burn was the paper and half a box of matches. Forced to face the reality that nobody was coming, she cooked herself a hot dog on the stove in the cabin, and she decided to lay back and watch the stars.

It would be nice to have a friend while she was here, but Katie wasn't about to let the lack of friends equal a lack of fun. No way. She was used to spending time alone. Besides, Bill would be here tomorrow, or the day after. She hadn't seen her father in nearly a year. They would have lots to do once he got here. Still, it wasn't the same as having a friend her own age.

"Are you sleeping or just dreaming?" Katie jumped at the voice. She hadn't heard anyone approach. She sat up and stared at the dark haired boy. "If you aren't going to say anything," Pete teased. "Perhaps we should leave."

Katie tried to see beyond Pete to the steps. "We?" she queried. "All I see is you."

"That's because the others are out front by the fire."

"What fire? I couldn't get one going."

"Shaun lit it." Katie looked at him askance. He explained. "You met him at the beach." When Katie stared at him with a dumb look on her face, he added, "the guy with red hair."

"Oh, Red. I didn't know his name. He never told me."

"Red fits. I've often called him that myself. Anyway, Red lit the fire, and a few of our friends have already gathered. Are you going to join us or do we party alone?" He walked over and offered his hand to Katie. "What's it going to be?"

Katie accepted his hand, and let him pull her to her feet. "So, Red lit my fire." She was stalling. She was still having a hard time believing Pete was here. That any of them were here.

"I'm sure Red would like nothing better than to light your fire." Pete winked at Katie. She felt the heat creep up her neck to her ears, and knew her face was as red as Shaun's hair. "He's done nothing but talk about you since this afternoon. Katie this. Katie that. I'd watch him if I were you." Katie was thankful for the cover of darkness. It felt like her cheeks were on fire. "Found her," Pete called as they rounded the corner, and stepped off the deck. "She was sleeping out back."

"Was not," Katie retorted. "I was watching the stars."

"I know. That's your story and you're sticking to it."

Pete opened a nearby cooler, and tossed Katie a can of beer. The action startled her, and she nearly missed it. Everyone laughed. Katie was about to toss it back when she realized everyone else had a beer. She didn't want them to think she was a baby and leave, so she decided to keep it.

She thanked Pete for the beer, and checked out the others. She had seven visitors in all. There were five boys, counting Red and Pete, and the boy from the deck, and two girls. She hadn't seen the two girls or the one boy at the beach earlier. "Hi. I'm Katie," she said, nodding slightly to acknowledge the ghost. As long as he was going to hang around, there was no sense trying to ignore him.

The small, blonde sitting nearest Katie raised her beer can in greeting. "Patty," she said. "And this is Marc." She indicated a boy with short, sandy colored hair sitting next to her, who also raised his can in acknowledgement. Katie recognized him from the winning team at the beach.

"Brenda," the girl sitting beside him nodded. She had dark hair. It was hard to tell in this light, but it looked almost black. Katie wondered how long it really was. It hung past the log she was sitting on, and it was in a braid.

Beside Brenda sat Red. He raised his can in greeting, and blew a kiss to Katie. He wore a stupid grin on his face making Katie wonder just how many beers he had before coming here.

She quit thinking about Red the moment she saw *him.*

He sat across the fire from her. His alabaster skin glowed in the flickering firelight. Then he turned his deep, penetrating eyes her way, and everything else ceased to exist. Katie was drawn to him like a bee to a flower, unable to tear her eyes away.

Of their own accord, her legs carried her to where he sat. This boy definitely wasn't at the beach earlier. His lips parted in a smile to reveal even white teeth, and then he spoke a single word. "Jack."

Katie felt her own smile widening in response. "Katie," she choked out past the lump in her throat.

"So you mentioned." He made room on the log between Red and himself. "Would you like to sit down, Katie?"

With the simple invitation awareness returned. No longer was she alone in the universe with the man of her dreams. She was plain old Katie, acting a fool in front of a group of strangers. *Face it girl*, she berated herself. *You were practically drooling over him.* When she finally got the courage to glance around she realized nobody was paying attention to her. They were watching Brenda, who was now holding a guitar Katie hadn't noticed before. Katie let a sigh of relief escape, and quickly sat between Jack and Red. She watched silently as the boy from the deck tried to get Pete's attention, and then sat on a nearby log, scowling.

Brenda was strumming the guitar now. A quiet, soothing tune and Katie allowed herself to relax and enjoy the unexpected treat. It took a few moments before she realized that Red was speaking. "I'm sorry. What did you say Red, uh Shaun?" *Please don't notice the slip.* He did.

"Red's fine," he slurred. "Lots of guys call me Red. Not that I think you're a guy," he hastily added. He tipped the can, and drained his beer. "Want another?" he asked, wiggling the can to be sure it was empty.

Katie jiggled her own beer can slightly. She could hear the liquid sloshing inside, and hoped nobody else noticed that she hadn't taken a drink. "I'm fine. I've still got lots."

Jack chuckled quietly. "Of course you have lots," he leaned closer, and whispered conspiratorially. "It's hard to run out of beer if you don't open the can."

Way to go, Katie, she berated herself silently. *You could have at least opened the can.*

Jack reached down, and took the beer from her trembling fingers. "No sense opening it now. It's probably warm. Here let me get you a cold one."

Katie watched him reach into the trunk of the car parked in front of the cabin. She hadn't noticed the car earlier, which said a lot about her powers of observation. She hadn't even heard a car while she was out back.

Jack returned and handed her a can of orange soda. "I hope this will do?" He spoke almost in a whisper. "It was this or beer. And you don't seem too interested in beer."

Katie smiled, grateful for the pop. "This is perfect," she said as she popped the top.

"What's that?" Red once again leaned towards Katie. "Let me taste that." He slurred as he grabbed for her pop, only to have Jack knock his hand away before he reached it. "Aw, Jack," whined Red. "I only wanted a taste."

"Maybe you should just stick with what you have."

Red looked at Jack, then Katie, and then back to Jack before sitting back in his seat, a scowl on his face.

Brenda was playing a more popular song now, and the others were singing along. Nobody was paying any attention to Red, Katie, and Jack. Even the dead boy was watching Brenda, but Katie still felt as if someone, or something, was watching her. She couldn't suppress a shivered.

"Are you okay?" asked Jack. "Are you cold?"

"No. Not cold. Someone just walked over my grave." She giggled nervously, and took a long drink of the soda. "Thanks again." She tipped the soda can in an attempt to end the conversation. Luckily, Jack took the hint.

"I take it you don't like beer." It was a statement not a question.

"Not really. I stole a sip or two from my dad's beer when I was younger, but I didn't like the taste. Which is probably a good thing considering the drinking age back home is twenty one." *Great, I'm babbling again. Either I'm not talking or I'm talking too much, and I never say anything smart, or cute.* "What's the ...?"

"Where's home?" Jack asked at the same time. They both laughed. "What's the what?"

"Drinking age. Nobody here looks twenty-one. Home is Niagara Falls. Stateside."

"Nineteen and you're right. Nobody here is twenty-one. I'm the closest and I just turned nineteen today."

"Happy birthday. Is this supposed to be your birthday party?"

"Not really. The only reason we need to party is the weekend. Besides, I lied. It's not really my birthday. That was Tuesday." Jack took a sip of his beer, pulled a face and dumped the rest out on the ground. "Great stuff," his voice dripped with sarcasm.

"If you don't like it why do you drink it?"

"I don't know. I guess because I don't drink often, and it is the easiest thing. If I feel like a drink, I just have a beer now and again. I'm usually driving so I stick to soda. I can't afford do to get caught drinking and driving on my way back to town."

"Do you live in town?"

"No. I'm staying with my uncle. He's a detective. He helped get me a summer job at the police station."

"Are you going to be a detective too?"

"I'm studying forensic science."

"Oh." Katie wasn't sure what forensic science was. She thought it had something to do with blood samples, or was it fingerprinting? She wasn't about to show her ignorance on the subject by saying anything further. She would go to the library first and find out what it was. She changed the subject yet again. "If you don't live in town where do you live?"

"I'm not far from you actually. I live in St. Catharines. About two blocks from the falls." He picked up his empty beer can, and stood. "I'm going to get myself a soda. How's yours?"

Katie shook her can. "Good."

"Do you want a soda, Shaun?"

"No way. Get me a beer would you, Jack?"

Red slid closer to Katie and put his arm across her shoulders. He leaned so much he nearly knocked her off the log. "Is Jack bothering you?" he slurred.

Katie shrugged his arm off. "No," she told him. "Jack's not bothering me. But you are beginning to."

"Aw, Katie me girl," Shaun spoke with exaggerated brogue. "You cut me to the quick."

Katie almost smiled at his silliness but caught herself in time. She remembered what Pete had said about Red having a crush on her, and although she didn't want to hurt him, she didn't want to encourage him either. "I'm not your girl," she told him firmly, but gently. "I'm not anyone's, girl." She saw the hurt look in his eyes, and sought to change the subject. "I didn't think anyone was going to come tonight?"

Red laughed. "What? Not come, and miss a chance to be with you? Whatever gave you that idea?"

"Oh, I don't know. Maybe because of what happened on the beach."

"What happened on the beach?" Red seemed genuinely surprised.

Jack chose that exact moment to return with his soda. "Miss me?" he teased.

"No way. She didn't miss you." Red answered before Katie had a chance. "She had me." He draped his arm around her, almost as if he wanted to emphasize his claim on her.

Katie wiggled out from under Shaun's heavy arm. "I was just saying to Shaun, how I didn't think anyone would come tonight," she said, a little louder than she intended. The others quit singing to look at her, and Brenda put down her guitar.

"Why didn't you think we'd come?" asked Pete.

"Oh, I don't know. Maybe because the minute Daina mentioned the Outlook, everybody left. Before you could say Jack Spratt I was standing on an empty beach."

Pete actually looked embarrassed. Shaun still looked confused. "We didn't realize we left you alone," Pete said. "It's just, we used to party here a lot, but we haven't been back since last summer." The dead boy was staring at Pete, his eyes burning with intensity.

"Not since Rick died," explained Marc. "When you mentioned the Outlook it brought back memories. We didn't purposely leave you in the dark, so to speak."

"Rick was my best friend," continued Pete, almost as if he were being compelled to speak by the dead boys, Rick's, stare. "We grew up together in Dreswell. We'd been coming here every year since we were five. Last year there was an accident, and he died. At least that's what the police say, but I don't believe it was an accident."

"What happened?" Katie asked, although she was afraid she already knew the answer.

"We were all drinking. It didn't seem so at the time, but Rick must have drunk a lot more than the rest of us. He fell." Jack said the words, but Katie had the feeling he didn't believe them either.

He's hiding something, she thought. She was positive there was something he didn't want the others to know. Something he was keeping from them.

"He fell from the porch out back," he said. Rick's glowing eyes were now on him, as if he could force him to say something.

Rick turned pleading eyes on Katie. "Help me," he said.

I can't help you. Katie threw the words at his specter with her mind. *You're already dead.*

Katie felt as if someone had kicked her in the gut. She grabbed her stomach and bent over, moaning. She stared into the fire, and saw it all again. *Rick leaning on the railing, while the shadow moved menacingly toward him. Rick as he plummeted to his death. Her standing on an old scarred deck, and leaning against a brand new railing.* "No," she moaned audibly, unaware she had done so. There had been no accident. Pete and Jack were right, and she had to find a way to show them the truth.

"Are you okay, Katie?" asked Brenda, her voice full of concern. She came around the fire and put her arm around her comfortingly. "Look what you've done, Jack. Why did you have to tell her Rick fell from her deck? It's bad enough knowing that the person who used to stay in your cabin has died, forget that he died there."

"I'm ok," Katie insisted. "What exactly happened?" If she were going to help, she would have to know everything.

"We were partying." Pete began the story. "It was the last week of July, last year. Rick's parents were visiting some friends in town and we had the place to ourselves. Clouds completely hid the moon. I remember thinking it was the darkest night of the summer. We built the fire so high we were afraid it might catch the trees. There was an awful lot of beer that night. Rick drank most of it himself. He was upset because he and Daina had a fight."

"Daina and Rick were a couple then," interjected Patty.

"Yeah," Pete said his voice full of derision. "Daina and Rick were a couple. Or so Daina wanted to believe."

"That's not fair, Pete," said Patty. "Just because you don't like Daina."

"And I suppose you do?"

"Well I don't dislike her if that's what you're implying. I feel sorry for her."

"Why? Because she goes around telling anyone who will listen that her one true love is dead. That's a crock. You don't know her. Daina lives in a fantasy world. She wouldn't know the truth if it jumped up and slapped her in the face. And that is exactly what happened the night Rick died."

A twig snapped in the woods behind Katie. She turned but couldn't see anything. It was too dark and the trees were too thick. Yet, she knew someone was out there. Someone or something. Shuddering, she turned back to the fire.

"As I was saying," continued Pete. "Rick and Daina had a fight. It was obvious to everyone, except Rick, that Daina wanted to be his girlfriend. She was always following him around like some little lost puppy, clinging to his every word. At first, Rick thought it was cute. However, that night he'd had enough and told her to leave him alone. She went ballistic. 'She was screaming like a banshee,' Rick said. Cursing him up and down. Accusing him of leading her on. He couldn't understand what her problem was. He had a girlfriend back home. He'd never made any secret of it. In fact, he was always bemoaning the fact that they couldn't spend the whole summer together. But for some reason, Daina set her sights on Rick. It wasn't as if they ever went on a date. Sure, they hung around. We all did. We were a gang. We played volleyball together. We went swimming together. We went to the movies together. Always together as a group. Not once did Rick go anywhere with Daina that the rest of us didn't go. Tell me?" he asked of no one in particular. "Does that sound to you, like the actions of a true love?"

Nobody answered, but Pete didn't expect anyone to. He continued. "Rick was my best friend. I knew he was drinking excessively that night, but I didn't try to stop him. Nobody did. Then around midnight we all left. I, for one, was still in trouble for breaking curfew the week before. I knew my folks would kill me for being late again, and I didn't want to risk it. Looking back, I wish I had. At least then, Rick might still be alive. "Anyway, we left just before midnight and Rick was alive then. I tried to get him to go inside, but he refused. 'I'm staying right here until morning,' he said."

Pete started to take a drink of his beer, hesitated, and then threw the can into the fire. "Damn him. Why did he have to drink so much? Why did he leave the fire? Why did he die?"

Brenda put her arms around Pete, comforting him the same way she comforted Katie earlier, and continued the story. "As Pete says, we left Rick by the fire that night, but that's not where his parents found him. The first thing Mrs. Mathers did was go to Rick's room to check on him. She always did that when they came home late. Rick told us once that it drove him crazy. 'How am I supposed to sneak out at night if she's always checking on me,' he complained. Anyway, he wasn't in his room and Mrs. Mathers tried to get Mr. Mathers to go out and look for him. 'He's probably off somewhere with Pete and forgot the time, as usual,' Rick's dad said. Mrs. Mathers said she had a feeling that something was wrong and she insisted he go look for Rick. That was when the moon broke through the clouds and lit up the broken railing on the deck."

Pete picked up the story again. "Mrs. Mathers rushed outside. Mr. Mathers was right behind her. She almost fell off the deck in her haste. When she got to the edge, she had to force herself to look down. That's when she saw the broken, bloodied body of her only child. Her screams could be heard all around the lake that night."

Jack took up the story then. "The police investigation didn't take very long. The railing was already cracked. Rick had been drinking. We knew that. We didn't need the autopsy to prove it. The official verdict was accident. It was clear-cut to the authorities. Rick had too much to drink, and while staggering into the cabin he lost his balance, crashed into the railing and fell. He broke several other bones, but the official cause of death was a broken neck."

"He wasn't that drunk," insisted Pete. "There is no way Rick's fall was an accident."

"And what's the alternative?" asked Brenda. "Murder? Suicide? Neither of those options is feasible."

Everyone was silent. What could they say? Like Katie, they knew deep down that someone was responsible for Rick's untimely demise. She was grateful for the warmth of Jack's leg against hers. It helped to dispel the sense of foreboding beginning to seep over her.

As if he had only now noticed how close Jack was sitting, Shaun chose that moment to jump up and glare at the two of them.

"What are you doing, Shaun?" asked Jack.

"Me? What are you doing, Jack? Snuggling up to my girl like that. You're supposed to be my friend."

"I am your friend." Jack said soothingly, trying to placate Shaun.

"A friend wouldn't try to steal another guy's girl."

"I'm not your girl, Shaun. I told you that."

"You sure acted like you were my girl," he insisted, unreasonably. "Coming on to me at the beach."

Katie stood up so fast she sent Red reeling back to his own seat. She was shaking with anger. How dare he? She had done nothing of the kind. "I did not," she said angrily.

"Oh, you did all right. You were flirting from the moment I saw you. Flashing your big, blue eyes at me."

Katie stared at Shaun through a red haze. A haze so thick she could barely see him. She spat out the first words that entered her mind. "Eat dirt and die, you jerk," she shouted.

Everyone laughed. "Way to go, Katie," someone said. "Let him have it."

Slowly voices penetrated the red fog. Katie's anger disappeared as suddenly as it came, and she was mortified. What had she said? "Oh, no." She covered her mouth as the words came back to her. Her eyes were wide with disbelief. How could she have said that? Red was drinking. He didn't know what he was saying. So he was a jerk, he still didn't deserve that. "I'm sorry, Red. I didn't mean it." She stepped towards him placating and realized Jack was holding her arm. Great, she thought. He probably thinks I'm going to deck the poor boy.

"Yeah, yeah," Red muttered. He looked around at everyone watching them, threw his arms up in the air, and said, "It's always hard for the chicks to control themselves around me."

Katie rolled her eyes, and then laughed. "Must be it."

Everybody laughed then. Jack looked at his watch. "It's almost midnight, people. I have work in the morning. Come on, Red. I'll drop you off on the way out. Anybody else for a ride?" The others were putting Red in the car when Jack turned back to Katie. He seemed worried about something. "Are you going to be all right alone, Katie? If you want, you can come home with me. I'm sure Aunt Shirley won't mind if you spend the night on her couch."

Go home with Jack. Now there was an intriguing idea. "I'll be fine," Katie told him. "I've stayed alone before," she lied. "Besides, I haven't been drinking."

Five

KATIE TOSSED ANOTHER pot of water on the fire, and stirred the ashes. She didn't want the fire spreading while she slept. At least that's what she told herself. The truth was she did not want to go in the cabin just yet. She might be able to convince those close to her that she didn't believe in ghosts, but she knew they existed. It was one thing to see them wherever she looked. It was another to have them talk to her. What did Rick expect her to do? She knew something horrible had happened the night Rick died. Something the others didn't know about, even if they had their suspicions. Jack said Rick died because he drank too much and lost his balance. That was a more believable story than one of murder. She had a hard time explaining what she saw to herself, never mind anyone else.

She wished Bill were here. He would know what to do next. Besides, although she didn't want to admit it even to herself, she didn't want to be alone. Anytime her parents went out without her, they left Matt with her. She would even settle for Matt right now, because with Matt around there was never time to think. Tonight there was no little brother. Tonight she was alone.

The wind kicked up, and clouds covered the moon, leaving her in darkness. It was darker than Katie would have believed possible after all the stars earlier in the evening. Maybe you couldn't see the stars as well back home because of the city lights, but those same lights helped keep the night at bay.

She was shivering steadily now. Soon she would need to go and get a sweater. Once inside she would as likely as not stay inside. It would be warm inside. She could curl up with a good book and forget about Rick and tales of murder.

A deafening clap of thunder echoed over the lake. A simultaneous flash of lightening lit the path between the fire pit and the door. Katie never hesitated. Her legs moved of their own accord, and she reached the front door as the first big drops hit. Katie had no time to worry about ghosts now. The patio doors were open and so were several windows. The clouds burst as Katie slid the doors home. She leaned against them, panting.

That settles it, Katie thought. I can't possibly go back outside in this. She locked the doors and closed the windows. In her bedroom, she shuffled through the books she brought with her. She settled on Calvin and Hobbes. Surely, she could count on them to banish all ghosts. Ten minutes later, her laughter came out a small shriek. Thunder shook the cabin. The light went out.

"Calm down, Katie," she said aloud, while feeling around for the lamp. She turned the button. Nothing. She tried again. Still nothing. "Blown bulb." Katie set her book beside the now useless lamp, and felt the wall between the bed and the door for the switch. Her fingers found their target. With a sigh of relief, she flicked the switch. The room remained in darkness. Outside the thunder continued to rumble. The intermittent flashes of lightning her only source of light.

"Great. The storm must have knocked out the power. And me with no candles." Katie kept talking to herself. The sound of her voice at least helped to dispel the cloying darkness. "Maybe there are candles in the kitchen." She was about to step into the hall when another clap of thunder shook the cabin. With a squeal, Katie turned and jumped into bed. She pulled the covers up over her head. I'll look for candles in the morning, was her last thought as she drifted into dreamland.

A rapping woke her a few hours later. It grew louder, more persistent. Katie couldn't shut out the sound. It would not let her go back to sleep.

"Katie." Apprehension filled her at the simple sound of her own name. "Katie. Help me, Katie."

Slowly she pulled back the covers and sat up. Something was wrong. The room was awash with light. A sickly green light. She could see everything clearly, as if it were day. Her book lay on the bedside table at the base of the lamp. She reached over and turned the button. The lamp remained as useless as it had been when she went to sleep. She continued to look around the room. Wide, frightened eyes stared back from the mirrored dresser at the foot of her bed. The closet door stood slightly ajar. Did she leave it open? She couldn't remember. The room seemed to be exactly as it was when she went to sleep—yet something was different.

It wasn't just the green tinge to the room. It was the silence. The room was as silent as a tomb. Her tomb.

"Katie. Help me, Katie." The disembodied words hung in the air, filling the room with foreboding. Katie swallowed the lump in her throat. On shaky limbs, she glided toward the window. Her arms moved against her will.

She opened the curtains.

Shaun floated in front of her. Dead, accusing eyes stared in at her. His mouth moved as if to speak. Words, mixed with decaying leaves and dirt tumbled from the orifice. "Help me, Katie," he said. "Don't let this happen."

Lighting filled the room.

Her scream was lost in the thunderous roar of the raging storm.

Six

THE CACKLE OF crows dragged Katie to the edge of wakefulness, and then pushed her over. A gentle scratching filled the room. Katie stared at the window. Trepidation made her heart pound faster and breathing difficult. Jumbled memories fought for supremacy.

Katie was facing Red by the fire through a red haze. "Eat dirt and die," she told him.

Red with his mouth full of dirt, and his dead eyes accusing. "Don't let it happen," he pleaded. "Help me, Katie."

Katie suppressed a shudder, and forced herself to approach the window. Cautiously she drew back the curtains. A long branch from a nearby cedar rubbed the pane making a small scratching sound on its journey.

Suddenly the room was awash with light. A cleansing light that washed away the horrors of the night before. Katie's breath escaped in a long sigh of relief.

This was reality. The sun shining. The birds singing.

Last night was a nightmare.

Katie headed for the bathroom. A shower was just what she needed to wash away the evidence of a tormented night. She turned the shower knob.

Nothing happened. No water came gushing out. No gurgling sounded in the pipes. There wasn't even the slightest hum of the motor running. Katie tried the lights only to discover there was still no power.

"The pleasures of camping," she said, her voice dripping with sarcasm. There was no way she could shower now.

Katie pulled the brush through her tangled hair and grimaced at her reflection. Her blue eyes had their own luggage. Her coffee colored hair hung limply over her shoulders and her lips were much too large for her pale face. At least her nose wasn't too big. If only it didn't come to such a point at the end. Elf nose. That's what her mother called it. Katie would have preferred a human nose.

She continued to stare at her face critically, and couldn't help wondered how others saw her.

Katie wiped a trickle of sweat from her forehead and opened the window. The smell of fresh washed pine filled her nostrils. She hurried to open the rest of the windows, letting the breeze cool the rapidly warming cabin.

She slid open the deck doors and stood in awe before the view. The trees sparkled as a myriad of sunbeams danced along their branches. The lake sparkled like diamonds in the distance. She couldn't deny the pull of its beauty. She might not be able to shower, but she could swim.

Quickly she changed from her snoopy pajamas to her swimsuit, pulled on her shorts, shoved some money in her pocket, and pulled on her sneakers. Now she was ready for the climb down the hill. It would be faster than the road.

The carpet of pine needles, still wet from the storm, made the path treacherous. Katie slid past two trees before catching the branches of a third, and bringing herself to a sudden stop. Maybe this wasn't such a good idea after all. The path was a lot slipperier than she had expected. She looked up the hill to the cabin. It wasn't that far away. Maybe she should go back and follow the road?

She had only taken two steps when she began to slide backwards. Katie fell to her knees and tried to grab at the ground, but couldn't grasp anything solid. Trees flashed past. Katie managed to roll herself over. It was like sledding without a sled or snow. Katie bent her knees and dug her heels in. She let her pent up breath out in a huge gulp when her skid ended, just short of the shoreline. This definitely was faster than the road, albeit more painful. She brushed needles and dirt from the seat of her shorts. Her knees were dirty and sore. There didn't seem to be much damage, but she definitely had to clean up some before anyone saw her.

Unlike the beach where they swam yesterday, the shore here was rocky. The rocks stopped just in the water. Katie gasped as the water stung the tiny scratches on her legs. She took a few more steps. Muck clutched at Katie's bare toes in an attempt to suck her in. Grimacing she scrambled back onto the shore. She sat on a boulder and washed the muck from her feet, checking carefully for leeches and other creatures of the slime. Satisfied she didn't have any leeches stuck to her she pulled on her sneakers, and headed toward the beach.

The further she travelled along the water's edge the sandier it became. When she reached the edge of the trees, it was all sand. Katie pulled off her sneakers and once again tried the water. The cool water acted as a salve on her scratched legs, stinging at first then soothing. She dug her toes into the sandy bottom and let the granules cover them.

There was nobody on the beach or in the water this early in the morning, and Katie took advantage of her solitude. Tossing her shoes on the beach, she struck out for the raft. The water was refreshing. It made her feel clean and alive.

From her seat on the edge of the raft, Katie studied the shoreline. The beach was a good hundred feet wide. There was a picnic table under some trees to her left. To her right there were several boats tied to a dock, and a couple of boats pulled up on the shore, and tied to trees. Their ropes lay along the sand like silent snakes ready to strike.

One rope in particular drew her attention. It pulled tighter than the rest and lifted off the ground. She thought she could see something caught in the rope near the bow. It looked like a shoe. Katie felt sick. Her throat was tight, and she found it difficult to swallow. She swam to shore coming out of the water beside the boats.

Katie looked at the rope that held the boat. She was sure the sun was playing tricks on her. A shoe was tangled in the rope.

Tangled and twisted, a foot still inside. A blue-jean clad leg was twisted sideways hanging from the rope. It lay still.

This was a nightmare. It had to be. She was still asleep. She only dreamt that she woke up this morning. This is a dream. She repeated the litany even as she stepped over the rope, and rounded the front of the boat.

Wild red hair floated on top of the water. He shouldn't lie in the water like that, with his face down. It wasn't natural. She had to force herself to go near him. Each step was like walking in quick sand. Her feet were growing heavy, and she wanted to turn back, but she couldn't leave him like that. Even if this were just a dream, she couldn't leave him. Katie squatted beside him.

Gently, careful not to cause him any pain, she turned him over.

Red stared up at her. His face was blotched and bloated; his glassy eyes were wide with accusation. His mouth was full of decaying leaves and sand—yet she heard his words as clearly as she had last night.

"Help me, Katie," he said. "Don't let this happen."

Seven

SHE WAS STILL screaming when strong fingers gripped her shoulders. "Come away from there, girl," the strange voice said. "Come on. Get up from there. There's nothing you can do for him." Two strong hands lifted her to her feet. Her legs were wobbly, and she was grateful for their strength still holding her. "Call the police, Sam." The voice continued talking behind her.

"Phone's out, Frank. Has been all night. Tree fell on the wires, again."

"Then go find Pete Mitchell. He has a two-way in his shed. He can raise the cops on that. If not, drive to town. Just get the cops here. Fast."

The pressure on Katie's shoulders increased. She allowed them to turn her from the sight of Red's body. "It's just a dream. It's just a dream." She kept muttering, unaware she spoke aloud.

"I'm sorry," the strange voice spoke again. "Was Shaun a friend of yours?"

The simple words 'was Shaun a friend of yours' hit her with the power of a sledgehammer. This was no nightmare. She wasn't going to wake up from this one.

The sun no longer had the power to warm her. She was cold. Cold and empty. Did she cause this? Was she responsible for Shaun's death? The possibility was unbearable, but what could she have done? She didn't want to be responsible. She let them lead her to the picnic table, not paying any attention to her surroundings. She couldn't get the image of Shaun out of her head.

Katie stared out across the lake with unseeing eyes. She wasn't even aware when the man they called Sam returned. She was oblivious when Frank returned to the body. Nothing broke through the wall of ice that encased her.

"Katie. Are you all right, Katie?"

The voice reached her on some level. It had a ring of familiarity about it. Katie was too tired to bother turning towards the speaker. She let the voice drift away.

"Take her to her cabin, Daina."

"What about the police? Won't they want to talk to her?" On some level, Katie heard the disappointment in Daina's voice. *Was she disappointed they were letting her leave?*

"She's in no shape to talk to anyone right now. Take her to her cabin." The voice was firm, the voice of authority.

Katie felt pressure on her arm, and rose to follow Daina. Small, sharp stones cut into her bare feet, but she barely noticed. Even if she had, it wouldn't have mattered. Nothing mattered.

Red was dead. It was her fault. Never again would he play volleyball with his friends, swim in the lake, or sit around a campfire drinking beer and being obnoxious. He was dead— and it was Katie's fault. She should have done something.

The tears came then. Large, scalding tears. Like acid running down her cheeks, burning the memory of what she had seen forever into her young heart. She sensed Daina's condemnation even though she hadn't spoken a word. Daina thought Katie had something to do with Shaun's death. Maybe she did, but she wasn't the one who had killed him. She realized that. By the time they reached the Outlook, Katie was once again under control.

Katie changed into shorts and a tank top, before curling up on the end of the couch, her feet tucked beneath her. Daina sat on the chair across from Katie. She sat like a statue, offering no words of comfort, but Katie was grateful for her presence. Anyone else might have wanted to talk, and Katie wasn't ready for that yet. There would be time enough to talk later.

She knew the exact moment that the police arrived. The crunch of gravel beneath the car's tires was all the warning she needed. Daina jumped up and ran to the window. "It's the police," she said, relief evident in her voice. "I have to go now." Before the knock came at the front door, Daina left through the back.

"Miss Davis?" The officer looked up from the pad he was carrying.

"Actually it's Williams. Katie Williams."

"I'm sorry. Is Miss Davis here?"

"That'd be me. Katie. My father is Bill Davis, but my step dad adopted me. My name is Williams, not Davis." The officer quickly scribbled on his pad. Katie stepped back from the door. "Would you like to come in, Officer?"

"Black," he supplied his name, but hesitated before entering. I should have asked his name before inviting him in, thought Katie. Maybe I should have asked for I.D. but who else would be wearing a warm uniform today. She wiped the sweat from her brow, and led the way to the living room. "Have a seat," she said. When he sat on the sofa, she chose a chair opposite him, and waited for the officer to begin.

"There are a few questions I need to ask you, Katie. First, is your father here?"

"No. Not at the moment he isn't."

"Is there anyone else you would like to call?"

"Like a lawyer, you mean?" Katie twisted her hands nervously in her lap. Did she need a lawyer? Did he think, as she had in the beginning, that she was somehow responsible for Shaun's death?

Officer Black's next words alleviated her fears a little. "Actually, I was thinking more along the lines of your mother or father?" He grinned at Katie's obvious relief. "Unless you think you need a lawyer?"

Katie noted the twinkle in Officer Black's kindly blue eyes. She sat back in the chair, and made herself comfortable. "I don't need a lawyer." The words came out a little surly, and she grimaced. "I didn't do anything," she added.

"It's settled then, no lawyers. Will you call your mother?"

"My mom's in Algonquin Park with my stepdad, Luke, and my little brother."

Officer Black looked around uncomfortably, and began to fidget with his pen. "When will your dad be home?"

"I'm not really sure. There was a problem with his plane," she lied, not wanting the officer to think her father cared more about a story than his daughter. "A faulty part or something," she quickly added. "If they've fixed it, he will be here today, tomorrow at the latest. He called me yesterday from the airport." It was the truth. He had called from an airport.

"Perhaps we should wait until your father arrives. He can bring you to the station and we'll continue this interview there."

Katie was on the edge of her seat. "No." She nearly shouted. "Do it here. I don't want to go to the police station."

Officer Black leaned forward. He patted her hand in a fatherly fashion. "It's okay, Miss Williams. We can do it here if you like. I just thought you might be more comfortable if your father were with you. Is there anyone else I could contact for you?"

Katie instantly thought of Jack. She liked him. Trusted him. And he worked at the police station. He would be perfect. Then she rejected the idea as quickly as she had it. What would she say? Yes. There is someone. He's friendly, kind and the most magnificent sample of manhood I have ever come across. Oh, and he's smart too. He works at the police station. You probably know him. His name is Jack. How many Jacks could possibly work at the police station? Hundreds. "There's nobody," she finally said.

Officer Black was staring at Katie, and she squirmed uncomfortably. He must have sensed her discomfiture. "I really can't question you without the presence of an adult." He leaned back on the sofa, clicking his pen open and closed, and then he leaned forward. "What about Mrs. Mitchell? Would you have any objection to Mrs. Mitchell standing in for your parents?"

When Katie didn't object, Officer Black made a call on his radio asking the person on the other end to call and have Mrs. Mitchell come to the Outback. When she arrived, and settled on the couch, Officer Black leaned back on the sofa, note pad in hand, and pen poised. "Well then. Let's get started, shall we? Did you see anyone on the beach this morning?"

"No. Just Shaun."

"You knew the boy?"

"I met him yesterday."

"When was the last time you saw him alive?"

"Last night. Around midnight. He was here with some friends. We were sitting around the fire. They all left together. Around midnight."

"Who were the others with you last night?"

"There was Pete. I met him on the beach earlier in the day with Shaun. The others I met last night. There was Jack. You might know him. He works at the police station."

"He's an officer?"

"No. It's a summer job. I'm not sure what he does. He's studying forensic science."

The officer scribbled on his note pad once again. "I know who you're talking about. The others, who were they?"

"I'm not really sure who they were. They sat on the other side of the fire from Shaun, Jack and me."

"But you were introduced." He phrased it like a comment, but Katie chose to answer it as if it was a question.

"Only their first names. I told you, I only got here yesterday. I don't really know who everyone is yet." Katie cringed as the officer once again scribbled in his note pad. If I hear that scratching pen one more time I'm going to scream, she thought. Her head began to ache and she was beginning to wish that Officer Black would go away. "There was Pete. I think he was a friend of Shaun's. They were together earlier at the beach. There was another boy, Marc, and two girls. I think their names were Brenda and Patty."

"Where can I find these other kids?"

"I don't know. Maybe you could ask Mrs. Mitchell, or her daughter, Daina. They know all the kids who camp here. They would know who they are."

"Did anything happen last night that we should know about? Maybe someone had an argument?"

He knows, thought Katie. He already knows what I said, and he blames me. Now she was being paranoid. There was no possible way Officer Black could know what happened last night. He did not think that Katie was in any way responsible for what happened to Shaun, and there was no reason for him to. Unless she acted so guilty, she drew attention to herself.

Katie forced herself to relax. She told him about the argument she had with Shaun. Someone from the campfire last night would be sure to mention it. She told him Shaun had been drinking. There was no harm in that, they would know as soon as they did the autopsy anyway. She told him how she had found Shaun's body when she had gone for an early morning swim. "I would give anything to take back what I said."

Officer Black scribbled a few more things on his note pad, closed it and stood up. "I think I have everything I need," he said. "And if I were you, I wouldn't blame myself for what happened. It might seem like it right now, but words don't have the power to kill." He seemed to hesitate for a moment. "Maybe I shouldn't be telling you this. The investigation isn't over, but it looks like your friend Shaun's death was an accident. According to his family, he runs every morning along the beach, between six and seven o'clock. It looks like he tripped over the guide rope for the boat, and hit his head on a rock in the water. He drowned before he ever regained consciousness. As far as we can tell so far, there is no sign of foul play." They walked together to the car. "If we do have any more questions," he told her before starting the engine. "I'll be in touch."

"Yeah," Katie said. "I'll be here." She watched as he, and Mrs. Mitchell drove down the road.

She had just started up the stairs when she heard her name called. She ignored the voice and continued up the stairs.

"Katie." The voice was louder now. "Wait a sec. We want to talk to you."

There were four of them. She remembered seeing them playing volleyball at the beach yesterday. Not one of them had come to the fire last night. She didn't have to wonder why they were here now. She knew.

She ignored the girl who had spoken, and focused on the only boy in the group. He was the smallest of the bunch. Blonde, almost white hair stuck out awkwardly from beneath the blue and white baseball cap he wore. His large, dun colored eyes seemed alien in his too pale face.

"Did you want something?" asked Katie. Her tone of voice wasn't very friendly. Then, again, she didn't feel very friendly right now. She could see the curiosity in their expressions and she didn't like it.

The boy began to shuffle his feet in the dirt. He stared at those same feet as if they were the most fascinating things in the world. Katie was beginning to feel sorry for him. She forced the feeling down. "Well?"

"No." The word came out on a rush of air. One of the girls pushed him. His head came up as he stumbled forward and Katie could see the fear in his eyes. Fear of her? Or of them? "I-I m-mean." The boy was so frightened he was stuttering. "They, we, heard you found Shaun."

"Really?" Katie drew the word out and glared at the boy. She couldn't help herself. She knew what these kids wanted. Details of her grisly find, and she wasn't about to give them anything. She owed Shaun at least that much.

"Is, he, really, dead?" He spoke more slowly, making his voice steadier.

"Yes. He's dead." Katie still spoke in clipped tones.

It was as if a dam had broken with her answer. Their questions flooded over her, threatening to drown her.

"Was it awful?"

"Was there lots of blood?"

"Did you touch him?"

"What was it like?"

There were only four of them, but their questions kept coming and coming. Katie wanted to scream at them to shut up and leave her alone. She opened her mouth. A sob caught in her throat. Her eyes burned with unshed tears. She refused to break down in front of these vultures. She covered her ears to keep out their unending interrogation, and hurried into the cabin. She slammed the door and leaned on it, almost afraid they would beat the door down to get at her. She could still hear them through the closed door.

"Come on," she heard someone say. "She's not going to tell us anything."

"What do you want to do?"

"I know. Let's go to the beach. Someone there will know something."

Katie waited at least ten minutes after she quit hearing their voices. She had decided to call her mom to come get her, and didn't want to run into them on her way to the phone. After several failed attempts, the operator informed her that the lines in Algonquin were still down. "I'm sorry," she told Katie. "Sometimes the lines are down for several days after a storm like the one we had last night. All I can tell you is to try again later. Perhaps they will be in operation by then."

Eight

KATIE WAS TRYING to read when there was a knock at the
door. Cautiously, she opened it a crack, wishing it had a peek
hole, and then flung it wide when she saw Daina standing on
the stoop. "Come in, Daina," she said, surprised at how happy

she was to see a familiar face. She hadn't realized just how isolated she felt, alone in this strange place.

"Hey, Katie." Daina's smile didn't quite reach her eyes. Katie put it down to the morning's events. "I can't come in. Don't have time. Mom sent me to bring you to lunch."

The mention of food reminded Katie how empty she felt. She hadn't eaten a thing since the night before, and thought that might have something to do with it. Then she remembered how many people had been in the restaurant the day before. She didn't want to sit there with all those people looking at her, and speculating about the girl who found Shaun. "I'm not really that hungry," she fudged.

"Oh, that doesn't matter. Mom said you'd try to beg off. I'm not to let you. Her words were 'don't take no for an answer'."

"But I'm really not hungry," began Katie, only to be interrupted by Daina.

"You don't have to worry about people staring, you know. We eat all our meals upstairs in our apartment. Besides, it'll just be you and me, and a couple of sandwiches. Mom never takes the time to have lunch with me. Dad's probably in the woods behind the tenting grounds. He spends most of the day there. They're clearing more sites, as if there's not enough to do around here now."

Katie was shocked at the bitterness in Daina's voice, but before she could speculate on the reason, Daina hurried on. "So, what do you say? Want to keep me company over a cold sandwich?"

Katie's stomach growled. She giggled to cover her embarrassment. "Sure. Just let me lock up." Daina rolled her eyes. Katie ignored her, and locked the door. She did not intend to come back to a cabin full of curious strangers.

Katie thought they would enter the apartment from the front of the office. She remembered seeing stairs the day before. She was wrong. Instead, they climbed a rickety old set of stairs, steep and narrow, at the back of the building. They belonged in a horror movie, the perfect setting for a battle between a monster and the hero, not on the back of someone's home. When they finally reached the top, the wind had picked up a bit. Katie was grateful to reach the top safely. She felt the stairs swaying in the wind, and there was a moment when she thought the stairs would pull away from the wall.

Daina's apartment was more spacious on the inside than it looked from the outside. It could have been the effect of the windows. Two sides of the living room were solid glass looking out at the lake. "This is great," she said. "What a view. I could stand here for hours."

"I used to think that, too." Daina was looking out a different window. "At least there was something to watch from this window." Her voice was bleak making Katie wonder what could make anyone sound so sad. "Look. From here you can see the Outlook."

Katie joined Daina at the side window. You could see the cabins along the ridge from here. Katie followed the curve of the road, counting to find her cabin. She could almost make out the deck.

Daina's voice was so low Katie could barely hear the words. "I'd sit for hours and just watch Ricky."

What was she talking about? You'd need a pair of binoculars to see anything from here, and even then, it would be iffy. "I can't," she began, but Daina continued as if she were alone in the room.

"I loved you, Ricky." Her words were barely above a whisper. Katie was sure she wasn't supposed to hear them. "Why did you leave me?" Suddenly Daina's voice grew louder, and angry. "You *shouldn't* have left me."

Katie backed away awkwardly. What should she do? What could she do? Obviously, Shaun's death had awakened

Daina's grief for her friend who died last summer. Daina was the same age as Katie. Katie had never even had a boyfriend. She couldn't imagine anyone his or her age being in love. According to Pete and the others, Ricky was not in love with Daina. They weren't even dating, according to Pete.

Katie wanted to leave. She didn't know what to do or say to help Daina. When the door behind them opened, Katie turned to greet Mrs. Mitchell with barely concealed relief.

"How are you doing, Katie? It must have been just horrible for you finding young Shaun like that. Don't you worry. It's all over now." Mrs. Mitchell swept into the room, and engulfed Katie in her plump arms, almost crushing the breath from Katie's lungs.

Katie managed to extract herself from Mrs. Mitchell's embrace, just as Daina threw herself into her mother's now empty arms.

"It's awful," Daina wailed. "Shaun was my best friend, and now he's dead."

Images flashed in Katie's mind, like a short video clip. *They were on the beach, and Shaun accidently threw grass on Daina. The look of hatred on Daina's face when she glared at Shaun made Katie shudder.* If Shaun was Daina's best friend, I sure wouldn't want to be her enemy, she thought.

"There, there." Mrs. Mitchell patted Daina's shoulder soothingly. "Let's have some lunch, and we'll all feel better."

They had just sat down to a plate of sandwiches when Mr. Mitchell walked in. "Hi, hon." he gave Maggie Mitchell a quick peck on the cheek, and winked at the two girls across the table. "How are the two prettiest girls at Beechwood Manor?" he asked as he sat down, and reached for a sandwich.

Katie felt herself blushing at the compliment. She thought Mr. Mitchell was being kind by including her, but still she felt uncomfortable. She was completely unaware of how others really saw her.

Daina, on the other hand, was basking in her father's unexpected attention. She tried to monopolize her father, glaring at Katie whenever Pete Mitchell tried to include Katie in the conversation. Neither Maggie nor Pete Mitchell seemed to notice anything out of the ordinary in their daughter's behavior. Katie began to wonder if she was imagining it herself.

"Did you find out anything, Pete?" asked Maggie Mitchell.

"I was talking to Jack." Katie's ears perked up at the name. Then she realized they weren't talking about the same Jack. "He says," continued Mr. Mitchell. "That Shaun's death

Final Justice

was an accident. Plain and simple. Shaun jogged along the beach, and tripped over the guide rope. When he fell, he hit his head on a rock and knocked himself out. He drowned before he ever woke up."

"That's not true!" Daina nearly screamed the words. "It wasn't an accident. Someone killed him."

Maggie Mitchell turned shocked eyes on her daughter. "What are you saying, Daina?"

"Think about it, Mom." Daina spoke to her mother the way one might an obtuse child. "Shaun ran on that beach, every day at the same time. Rain or shine. He knew where every boat was tied. He leapt over those ropes like a horse in a steeplechase. What makes you think he tripped this time?"

"Daina." There was a wealth of warning in the single word.

Daina chose to ignore her father's warning. "No, Mom. The cops are wrong. Shaun was punished, just like Ricky was."

Maggie shook her head sadly, and looked at her daughter with pity. "Daina, honey," she said soothingly. "You know Ricky's death was an accident. He was drunk and he fell against the railing. It was partly our fault, I know. We should have checked those railings more often. If we had, maybe Ricky would still be alive. That's something we have to live with every day of our lives. But he was *not* murdered."

89

Daina glared at her mother. "That's what you think? But I know different." For one very brief instant, Katie knew she spoke the truth. Then Daina smiled beguiling at her father, successfully wiping the frown from his face. "Pass me another sandwich please, Daddy," abruptly changing the subject.

They spent the rest of the meal in a completely different atmosphere. There was no more mention of either Shaun or Ricky. Pete Mitchell kept them busy with anecdotes of several different boys he had hired on over the years.

"My favorite was Michael. He kept us in stitches that summer."

"Tell Katie about the tables, Daddy," encouraged Daina.

"Ah. The tables. We decided to paint the picnic tables. I was sure Michael could handle such a simple task, so I left him to it. About three hours later I returned to find the tables done, but no Michael."

"Where was he?" asked Katie, knowing it was expected of her.

"Under a table. You see, he painted the tops of the tables first. Then, because the paint was wet, he couldn't turn them over to paint the bottoms. He had crawled underneath and there he was, laying on his back and painting the bottoms. When he came out, he was covered in brown measles."

Katie laughed so hard she nearly fell off her chair. The horrors of the morning effectively filed neatly away in a small corner of her mind, to be opened and examined, later, when she was alone.

After lunch, Daina asked Katie if she wanted to play basketball. "There's a net at the rec hall." At Katie's questioning look, Daina continued. "That's where we have dances on the long weekends."

Wow, mused Katie. *She sure runs hot and cold. One minute she's your best friend, the next she's staring daggers at you.* Katie debated going back to the Outlook, but she really didn't want to be alone. Besides, she liked basketball, and unlike volleyball she was good at it. She would just have to be careful that she didn't do or say anything to set Daina off.

Katie wiped the sweat from her forehead and plopped down on the grass, exhausted. "Whew, that was close."

"You can say that again." Dave sprawled on the grass beside Katie. "I don't know how you did it, but I'm sure glad you did." He was referring to the last basket Katie made.

Katie was proud of that basket. There she was jagging in and out amongst the other players, inching closer and closer to the hoop, when suddenly she came up against a brick wall.

At least it seemed that way. The guy was huge, and he really knew how to play ball. Katie had never come across anyone who could guard the way he did. When she finally decided that second place wasn't so bad, he fell for her feint. She never hesitated. Just took the shot, and made it. Oh yes, she was definitely proud of that shot. "It was pure luck," she said. "I had just about given up. Man, is that guy good."

"I know. We've never won against his team before." Dave looked at his watch. "I have to go. I promised my mom I'd watch Benny, that's my brother, while she does the shopping. He's only three, and a real terror in the store. Grabs everything. Mom always ends up with a lot more in the cart than she wants. Come on, I'll walk you home."

Daina glared at the two of them, but quickly looked away when she realized that Katie could see her. *Now what have I done,* Katie wondered. She decided to ignore Daina.

Dave seemed nice enough. He was funny, had dark eyes, and a great smile. What did it matter if his wasn't the face she imagined when she closed her eyes? The face she saw was more serious, with deep, fascinating eyes. *Man, do I have it bad*, she thought. *Snap out of it girl. You would think you had never seen a boy before.* "That would be great," she told him. She would enjoy the company on the walk back.

They chatted on the walk back, and the time passed quickly. Before they knew it, they were on the road with all the cabins.

"Which cabin are you in?" Katie asked.

A blush crept into Dave's face, and he was suddenly fascinated with the antics of a squirrel in a nearby tree. "I'm not exactly in a cabin," he finally admitted.

"Not in a cabin? Where exactly is your trailer then?" Katie asked suspiciously.

Dave smirked, and shrugged his shoulders. "We have a trailer on the beach road."

"The beach road," Katie squealed. "You have a trailer on the beach road, and your mother is expecting you. Whatever possessed you to offer to walk me home?"

"Truth?"

Katie sighed. She was not used to dealing with boys. "Yes, the truth." She really hoped that she wanted to hear this.

"To piss Daina off." He said it with such glee in his voice.

Great! It wasn't as if Daina and Katie were best friends, but Katie really did not want to make an enemy of the girl. Katie rolled her eyes, and Dave laughed.

When they arrived at the Outlook, there was a strange car in the driveway. It was empty.

"Dad." Katie ran to the cabin, completely forgetting Dave's presence when her father stepped out the door. It was Bill who reminded her Dave was there.

"Katie." He was plainly pleased to see her. He hugged her, then held her at arm's length, and spun her around to get a good look at her. "My, how you've grown. You're a proper young woman now. And who might this fine young gentleman be?"

Flustered, Katie turned to Dave. How could she have forgotten him there? She introduced her father, and politely thanked Dave for walking her home. She tried to hide her embarrassment behind good manners. After a short exchange with her father, Dave left to go look after his brother.

Katie spent the next hour telling her dad everything that had happened since she had spoken to him on the phone. Maggie Mitchell had already given Bill the gist of it when he picked up the spare key for the cabin. Now he let his daughter tell him everything, in her own words. He knew she needed to tell it—to help ease her anxiety.

Katie didn't say anything about the nightmare. She wasn't exactly sure it was a nightmare, and not an actual visitation. She felt bad that she hadn't been able to help Shaun. The truth was there wasn't really anything she could do for him, or for Rick. For once, she would like to be able to do something besides see and hear dead people.

Nine

THE SUNLIGHT WAS waning. Bill lit a fire in the pit, while Katie gathered more wood from the box under the stoop. Then he went shopping. They had decided on roasted hotdogs for supper. Katie had a feeling they were going to eat a lot of hotdogs, sausages, and anything else they could roast over the fire. Bill admitted he wasn't much of a cook, eating most of his meals at restaurants, and as for Katie, a few simple dishes—macaroni and cheese, hamburgers and fries—were her limit.

The fire drew them, like moths to a flame. Where last night, Katie didn't think anyone was going to show up, tonight she didn't think there was anyone who wasn't going to show. Except Daina and Jack. They were almost conspicuous in their absence.

Pete and Patty were the first to arrive. "I'm sorry about Shaun," Katie told Pete.

"I know, Katie." Pete blinked back the tears, and Katie felt guilty all over again.

"I feel like this is my fault," she said. "I behaved so badly yesterday."

"It's not your fault," Patty said. She casually threw her arm over Katie's shoulder, and gave her a quick hug. "It was an accident. It wasn't anyone's fault."

"Yeah, right. An accident." Pete didn't sound convinced, and Katie was reminded of Daina's earlier outburst. "Just like Rick was an accident. But Patty's right. You have no reason to feel bad."

Katie did feel bad, and she couldn't shake the feeling that she was somehow responsible. "The last thing I said to him," she began. Pete and Patty both interrupted her.

"We were all behaving badly," consoled Patty.

"It's Daina's fault, not yours." Pete scowled.

"Get real, Pete. How could this be Daina's fault? She wasn't even here." Patty was getting angry.

"She's the one who makes everyone crazy around here. You haven't been here very long." When Patty tried to interject, Pete hurried on. "You don't really know what Daina's like."

"Maybe not," insisted Patty. "But there's no way she's responsible for anyone's death."

Bill Davis chose that moment to return from the store, effectively ending their conversation. While Katie was introducing Pete and Patty, Marc and Brenda arrived. Katie was pleased to see that Brenda brought her guitar. "I don't go anywhere without it," Brenda said, with a self-mocking laugh. "I need the practice."

"Not from what I heard yesterday," Katie said, introducing the newcomers to her dad. "Brenda's the one I told you about. Wait until you hear her play. She's really good."

It was Brenda's turn to blush. Pete teased her for a second, and then let her off the hook by changing the subject. "I hear you travel a lot, Mr. Davis."

"Please, call me Bill. Mr. Davis makes me feel old," interjected Bill. Then, with a conspiratorial wink at Katie, "and I ain't old."

"Depends what you call old," teased Katie. Her father wasn't a bad looking man, she thought. He was medium height, with the beginnings of a paunch, but his hair was blue-black with no hint of grey, and he had what her mom referred to as smoldering, mahogany eyes. Katie didn't want to think of her dad as having smoldering anything, but she didn't think he would ever really look old.

Bill assumed a wounded expression, and clutched his heart. Everybody laughed. "In answer to your question, Pete. I presume it was meant as a question, and not just a way to give poor Brenda a break?" he didn't miss a thing, Katie's dad. "Yes, I do travel quite a bit."

Pete laughed. Katie's dad was neat. Most parents didn't joke around with your friends. They just looked at them as if they were from outer space, and then did something to embarrass you. "Maybe you can tell us about some of the places you've been?"

Bill reached into the still open car door, and pulled out a bag of groceries. "Let me put these away," he said with a grimace. "Then I'll tell you about a few of the places I've seen." He had gone to buy hotdogs, and ended up with six bags. Once he got to the store, he thought of buns, then mustard and ketchup to go on the buns, and then something to drink. He was walking past the meat counter, and the cold meats looked good. After picking up cold cuts, he realized they needed bread, butter, mayonnaise, salt, pepper, etc., etc. Before he knew it, he had bought out half the store. Maybe they should have just eaten at the restaurant.

"Here, let me help." Pete grabbed the bag, and handed it to Marc. Then he pulled the rest of the bags from the car, and handed them to the others. Soon everyone was carrying something into the cabin, except Pete and Katie's dad.

"Nice move," teased Patty, as she ran up the steps with a bag. "Maybe you can check the fire."

Soon they gathered back around the fire, and Bill began telling stories of his journeys. Nobody said a word. They were completely engrossed. At one point, Marc forgot what he was doing, and let his wiener burn. It looked like a hunk of charcoal, but he ate it anyway.

Dave and some of the others from the basketball game arrived. They waved at Katie, and found spots around the fire. If she hadn't seen them arrive, she wouldn't have known they were there. Someone passed around more wieners, and Bill continued to mesmerize them with his tales. Bill was a born storyteller, relating events in such a way that anyone listening felt as if they were a part of the action.

As Katie listened to her dad, she let herself relax. Her fears that she would be plagued with questions about Shaun evaporated. Everybody was too intent on what Bill was saying to worry about anything else. Faint rumblings in the north added sound effects to her dad's story of erupting volcanoes in Costa Rica. The wind whistling throughout the trees helped transport them to the Caribbean during the hurricane season. Even the acrid smoke burning their eyes helped set the scene for the burning rain forests of Southeast Asia.

Katie had heard the stories before, several times, but tonight it was as if she was hearing them for the first time. She found herself listening to the thunder in the distance, and imagining that it actually was the rumbling of a volcano. Katie wasn't the only one who screamed when the sky exploded with light and sound, and the clouds opened up on their heads.

Bill ushered them all into the cabin, and spent the next half hour driving them to their own homes. He was on his second run when Katie noticed Dave hovering around the door.

Katie caught his arm as he tried to slip out the door undetected. "Where do you think you're going?"

Dave shrugged. "Home," he hedged.

"Yeah, right." Katie eyed him skeptically. "If you're in such a hurry to leave, you could have gone on the first trip."

Dave kept his eyes anywhere but in Katie's direction. "There's no reason for your dad to have to drive us all home. It's not that far."

The wind chose that moment to blow a gust of rain in through the partially open door, nearly pulling it from Katie's hand. "Don't be stupid Dave. Your trailer is nearly at the lake. You'd have to be nuts to go out in this."

"She's right, Dave," Patty said. "There's no reason to be macho and walk home."

"I'm not being macho," argued Dave. "It's not that bad out there. Besides, I need to stop somewhere on the way home."

Dave grabbed Katie's arm, and pulled her through the door out onto the porch before anyone else could get in on the conversation, not that the porch was any protection from the rain that was blowing all around them. "Listen, Katie. I really can't wait for your dad. There's something I need to do on the way home."

"Like what. Get yourself killed. It's crazy out here. The way the trees are bent over, I wouldn't be surprised if they started to snap."

Dave pulled his collar up on his neck, and peered out at the storm. A few trees had bent nearly double in the wind, and some small twigs and leaves flew onto the porch. Katie was right. Anyone would have to be nuts to go out on a night like this, but if he didn't do it now, he wouldn't do it at all. "I'm not going to get lost, Katie. I've been camping here for years. I'll stick to the path, but I need to see somebody, and it can't wait until tomorrow." Without another word, he jumped off the porch and ran into the storm, ignoring Katie.

While Katie waited for her father to return from his last run, she marveled at how well the evening had gone. Not one single person had interrupted her dad's stories to bother her about Shaun, and she began to think she could put this entire dreadful day behind her.

Katie remembered her father often enjoyed a cup of tea in the evening. She found some amongst the groceries he bought, and decided to prepare him some, while she kept one ear open for the sound of his return. Tonight would be a perfect night to cuddle up to a good, hot, cup of tea.

The rain effectively drowned out the noise of the engine, but she distinctly heard the slamming of the car door and his steps as he ran up the stoop. She nearly jumped out of her skin when, instead of the door opening, somebody knocked. Who could possibly be here, now, and on a night like this? Her thoughts immediately flew to the police.

She removed the whistling kettle, and turned off the stove before opening the door to Jack. "Do you want tea?" she asked, more to cover her amazement at finding him at her front door than because she actually thought he might want some.

Katie ushered him into the kitchen, and finished preparing the tea. "Crumpet?" she asked, placing a plate on the table, unaware she had used her father's name for cookies. It made them sound more sophisticated he always said. "Dad got carried away with the shopping. He must have bought four different kinds, which is rather strange. Don't you think? I mean, I've never actually seen him even eat a crumpet." Katie rambled when she was nervous, and now was no different. She found it very hard to hide her relief when her father finally came back. It wasn't that she wasn't happy Jack had come for a visit. She was afraid he might realize how happy she was that he had.

"In the kitchen, Dad," she called, jumping up to pour his tea.

Bill hung his jacket over the back of a chair, and sat down. "Good, you found the crumpets." He grabbed one, and took a bite. "There's nothing like a good crumpet," he said.

Katie rolled her eyes skyward. Her father was acting as if it were an everyday occurrence to come home, and find a strange boy in the kitchen with his daughter.

"Jack, this is my dad, Bill Davis. Dad, Jack."

"Not *the* Bill Davis? Reporter extraordinaire?" It was the first time Katie had ever seen her father look uncomfortable, and she had a hard time hiding her grin.

"I wouldn't go that far," Bill began.

"I would," was Jack's answer. "I caught your report on the burning rain forests of Southeast Asia. I was riveted to my seat. Some of that footage. Let's just say it really opened my eyes. I can't imagine ever having to leave my home the way those villagers were forced to. And your exposé on the drug lords. If I have even half your detective skills I'll be the best cop ever."

"You should have been here earlier." Realizing her comment might sound like a rebuke, Katie hurried on. "Dad was telling us all about the rainforest fires tonight. You could almost hear the fire as it ate through the jungle, and the smoke. You could taste it."

"I would have enjoyed that, I'm sure." Jack drained his cup, and looked at Katie. She read the conflict in his eyes. A couple of times, while he was drinking his tea she thought he wanted to say something. Then he seemed to change his mind, or make up his mind at any rate. After several awkward moments, he stood abruptly, and again offered his hand to Katie's dad.

"It really is an honor to meet you, sir," he said. "And I'm sorry for stopping in so late." It wasn't that late. A quick glance at the clock told Katie it was barely ten thirty. "I just wanted to check, and make sure that Katie was alright."

"I appreciate your looking out for my daughter in my absence." Bill shook Jack's hand.

Katie escorted Jack to the door. "Thanks for the tea, Katie," he sounded distracted. "It was just what I needed to warm me." Katie watched him walk to his car. He had the driver's door open, when he turned abruptly, and faced Katie. "Be careful," he told her, before climbing in and slamming the door. "I don't want you to get hurt."

Ten

WHAT DID JACK MEAN? He didn't want to see her hurt. What was he trying to tell her? That he knew she liked him, and that the feeling wasn't mutual. Was she reading too much into the simple fact he had dropped by to see her after everyone else had already gone home? The questions chased each other around in her head, until finally, exhausted, she allowed sleep to claim her.

She sat straight up in bed, and listened. The wind howled like a banshee, and thunder blasted through the skies. Other than that, it was silent. Had she been dreaming?

Katie pressed her hand against her pounding heart, and willed it to slow down. Her heart didn't feel like it was a dream. Forcing sound past a throat constricted with fear, she called her father.

Bill came in, tying the rope around his housecoat. "What is it, Katie? What's wrong?"

Katie felt foolish now that her father was in her room. It was probably a dream. "I heard somebody scream, Daddy." Her own voice was small, hesitant, the voice of a child afraid she wouldn't be believed. The wind buffeted the trees outside her window causing them to moan and creak. Bill sat on the edge of her bed, and pulled Katie into his arms. He hadn't held her like that since she was five.

"It was only a dream, Katie," he assured her. "Probably brought on by a combination of the events of the past couple days, and the severity of the storm."

Katie shook her head with such fierceness she thought she would shake her own teeth loose. "I know what I heard,

Dad," she insisted, getting angry. "It wasn't the storm. It wasn't a dream. I heard someone scream."

"Could it have been an animal?" Bill asked.

Katie thought about what she heard. It could have been an animal. In fact, in could have been a dream. "You're probably right, Dad," she admitted. "It was probably either an animal, or a dream. I'm all right now."

"Maybe if you shut your curtains, it would help to keep some of the storm out."

Bill rose to close the curtains. Lightning flashed. Thunder crashed. Katie screamed. The limb of a large pine banged against the window on its journey to the forest floor.

A casualty of the storm.

The falling branch was the swansong of the tempest. The thunder moved off to the south, taking with it the lightning and the rain, and leaving a void in its wake.

Katie felt like she had just lost another friend. She glanced at the clock as she snuggled back into bed. Was it only ten after one?

Eleven

KATIE HELD THE covers over her head, but the banging just wouldn't quit. There was nothing else for it. She would have to get up, and take an aspirin. She'd never had such a pounding headache before, then again, she had never spent so many sleepless nights before either.

She did not want to move.

Katie groaned as the pounding grew louder, more persistent, only now it was accompanied by a voice. A heart wrenching, pain filled voice. "Katie. Open up, Katie. It's me. Daina. Please, open the door."

When she realized she wasn't dreaming, and Daina really was at the door, Katie hurriedly pulled her housecoat over her nightgown, and ran for the door. She just knew something awful had happened. Why else would Daina be here so early?

Her dad was already in the hall, a hysterical Daina sobbing in his arms, when Katie got there. "What's going on, Dad?" she asked.

Daina lifted her tear streaked face from Bill's shoulder, and boldly met Katie's gaze. "Who?" Katie forced the question passed her stricken throat.

"Dave." Katie felt the blood drain from her face, and a wave of dizziness had her clutching for the nearest wall. Her breath came in short, hard gasps, and her heart felt like it would leap from her chest. *Not Dave, too. This can't be happening.*

"But...he was just here...last night."

"I know." The words were innocent enough, but the look Daina gave her was accusatory.

How could she know that? She wasn't here last night. Katie had to admit, even to herself, that she could not have said who all was at the fire last night, but she would swear in a court of law, that Daina had not been there.

"What happened?" asked Bill, as he ushered Daina into the kitchen to sit down. "Would you make tea please, Katie?" Tea was Bill's first thought in any crisis involving kids over the age of five. Before that, it was toast and jam. Katie was thankful to have something to do as she busied herself with the kettle and tea pot.

"It was the storm last night." Daina sobbed. Although Daina had the right to be upset, Katie couldn't help but feel she was weeping crocodile tears for Bill's benefit. "When Dave wasn't home by midnight..."

"But that's not possible," interrupted Bill Davis. "When the storm hit I drove everyone home. It took five trips, but I made sure everyone was safe in their own place."

"Except Dave." Katie's voice was flat. She hoped she didn't look as guilty as she felt when her dad turned his questioning eyes on her. She cringed at the almost gleeful look on Daina's face. *She's really enjoying this,* thought Katie. *It doesn't matter that Dave's dead. She's enjoying putting me on the spot this way.* As soon as she let the thought enter her mind, Katie felt guilty. Of course, Daina was upset over Dave's death. She had known the boy for years.

"What do you mean, except Dave? Didn't I hear you say he was here last night?"

"Yes." Katie was speaking barely above a whisper now.

"Well?" Her dad wore a stern look on his face, probably his interviewing expression, and his voice was demanding. It clearly said, "Do not make me drag this out of you one word at a time."

Katie realized she was twisting the belt on her housecoat nervously. Quickly she dropped it, and swallowed. "Dave walked home," she blurted out. "He said you had too many people to drive home as it was. Besides, he said he had to go somewhere on the way."

"Did he say where he had to go that was so important that he would go out in a storm like that?"

"No." Katie knew the truth though. There was no doubt in her mind. Dave was going to see Daina last night, and Daina didn't want anyone to know about it. She also knew there was no way she would get anyone else to believe her— not without proof.

"How could you let him go out into a storm like that, Katie?"

Katie stiffened at the reprimand. "That's not fair, Dad. Several of us tried to stop him. I even warned him that going out into the storm could be dangerous. He wouldn't listen. He kept saying there was something he had to do. But he wouldn't tell anyone what it was." She took a deep breath. "Besides, what was I supposed to do? Tie him up?"

"You're right, Katie. It wasn't your fault. I'm sorry if I made it sound like I thought it was. He turned his attention back to Daina. "I'm sorry for the interruption. I don't usually allow myself to get distracted like that. Would you like a cup of tea?"

"No thank you, Mr. Davis. I don't drink tea." Daina lifted her tearstained eyes, and blinked a couple of times. "I would take a glass of water though, if you don't mind?"

Katie raised her eyes to the ceiling at Daina's obvious attempt to manipulate her dad. He wasn't really falling for this, was he? She handed Daina a glass of water. Daina took the glass, and snuffled, before telling Mr. Davis what she knew.

"When Dave didn't come home by midnight his dad was mad. Then he began to worry about Dave coming home in the storm. Marc and Dave usually hang together because their trailers are beside each other on the beach road, so he went to

Marc's trailer," she told them. "Marc told Mr. Martin, that's Dave's dad, that a bunch of the kids were up at your place last night, and that you drove them home around ten o'clock." Katie's dad acknowledged the truth of this statement with a nod, and Daina continued.

"Marc told Mr. Martin that almost everyone he knew was here last night, except me and Jack." Katie ignored the pout in Daina's voice, and met the accusing look in the other girl's eyes. It wasn't her fault that Daina wasn't at the fire last night, and she wasn't going to feel guilty about it. Daina shrugged, and lowered her eyes first.

"As I was saying, Marc couldn't remember whether Dave left before him or not. Next, Mr. Martin went to John's trailer."

Katie tried to picture him, but she wasn't sure which one was John. Daina continued. "Dave wasn't there either. That's when Mr. Martin decided to come here.

"I didn't hear anyone last night. Did you, Katie?"

"That's because Mr. Martin didn't stop," Daina continued before Katie could answer. "He said there weren't any lights on so Dave couldn't be here. He was taking the long way back, in case Dave was visiting one of the other trailers, when his headlights lit up something just off the road. When Mr. Martin stopped to investigate, he found Dave."

"What happened?" Katie whispered. She held her breath, and waited for Daina to answer.

"It looks like a branch broke in the storm. It fell, and hit Dave right on top of the head." A vision of Dave's dark features covered with scarlet floated in front of Katie's eyes. She covered her mouth, and ran to the bathroom. When she returned to the living room, she heard Daina say, "He died this morning, Mr. Davis. Mr. Martin called Dad from the hospital to let us know. Dave never woke up."

Twelve

"I'M GOING TO town, Katie. Do you want to come?"

The question startled Katie. She swallowed the last of her toast, and looked at him. "Is something wrong, Dad?" Her dad had been preoccupied since Daina left.

"I don't know, Katie. Something is going on here. I intend to find out what, and I could use your help."

"Just let me wash, and brush my teeth. I won't be five minutes."

Less than five minutes later, they were in the car heading for the nearest town.

A police car blocked the road, at the site where they found Dave. Bill drove on the grass opposite the site to get by. Curiosity had Katie turned half around in her seat, craning her neck to get a better look.

They had roped off at least a forty foot square with that wide yellow and black, plastic ribbon. The kind that had "DO NOT CROSS POLICE BARRIER," repeated on it. It didn't matter where you came across it you got the message. Katie could see six officers inside the barrier. They were walking slowly, their eyes on the ground.

Katie turned, and plopped back onto her seat. "What do you think they're looking for, Dad?"

"Evidence." Bill rolled down his window to let the warm, morning air fill the car. The sun was high, and it was already starting to get muggy. The temperature was primed to reach the eighties. If this heat kept up, they could expect another storm either tonight or tomorrow. "Fasten your seat belt, Katie," Bill reminded his daughter as they left the park.

The road was winding with several hills making Katie grateful that they didn't meet very many other vehicles. She laughed with delight when her dad pointed out a pair of mallards, with five ducklings, paddling around in a small roadside pond. Katie was the first to spot the fawn running back into the bush, and the only one to see the hawk circling overhead. Her dad said it was because he had to keep his eyes on such a treacherous road, but Katie teased him it was because he was going blind in his old age.

Soon there were more houses, and less wild life. They passed a liquor store, and a lumberyard, crossed a bridge, and entered the small hamlet of Felicity Falls. There was only the one road in and out. A small lake was on the north side, and all the houses on the south side. Ahead of them, at the end of the lake, Katie could see buildings on both sides of the road. By the amount of vehicles and people milling about, she assumed they were stores. This must be the main part of town.

"So, what's up, Dad?"

"Keep your eyes open for the local newspaper office. I believe its "The Felicity Cryer."

Of course, it was the Felicity Cryer. Her father probably knew not only the name of the paper, but the name of the managing editor, and most of the reporters as well. He made it his business to know these things. "Here, Dad." Katie had almost missed the small sign in front of an old house with a full front porch. She was expecting an office building, not this Gingerbread style, Victorian era home.

The outside of the house was a complete contradiction to the inside. They entered the foyer to find the reception area, complete with a secretary who was simultaneously talking on the telephone, and typing on a computer. Her smile was distracted, as she waved them toward a couple of armchairs to the left of her desk. They had barely sat down when she was standing over them.

"Good morning," she said, her hand outstretched. Her voice was brisk, yet friendly. "My name is Rhianna Burke. Is there anything I can help you with?"

They rose at the same time. Bill shook Rhianna's hand in greeting. Katie watched the woman carefully as her dad did the talking. "Hi, Rhianna. You don't mind if I call you Rhianna, do you? I'm Bill Davis, and this is my daughter, Katie." Bill kept eye contact with the woman the entire time, and his lips turned up slightly.

She's impressed, thought Katie. She knows who dad is and now she's wondering why he's here, in her town, at her newspaper office.

They may have caught Rhianna Burke off guard with this visit from famous investigative reporter, but she was enough of a professional to hide her surprise very quickly. She kept her face composed, and waited patiently for Bill to tell her what brought him there.

Bill's smile widened. Katie wondered how often he got women to do his bidding with that smile. "I was wondering if I could take a look at some of your back issues."

"Is there anything specific you're looking for?"

"No. Nothing specific," Bill hedged. He believed in playing his hand close to the chest. He believed the less people who knew what he was looking for, the better. He often found out more by going the long way around an issue. He chose that tack now. "I'm curious about the types of events that occur in a community of this size. You see," he forestalled her. "I'm thinking of buying a cottage here. A place I can bring the kids for vacations. Before I make any decisions, however, I want to find out what there is for kids to do around here."

Rhianna walked back to her desk, searched through one of the many drawers, then handed Bill a small pamphlet. "Here's a list of all the local events. Perhaps you'll find what you want in there." `And perhaps you won't' her eyes clearly said.

Katie wondered if Bill was actually reading the pamphlet, or just pretending for Rhianna Burke's benefit. He looked up at Rhianna Burke, and flashed that smile of his. "You know, Rhianna. I could probably get a better feeling about the different events if I could see the way the paper covered them. Some of these things, I'm not really sure what they are." He glanced at Katie, and winked. "Perhaps if we could see everything from last year. Say, June to Thanksgiving. That should cover it. Don't you think, Katie? I can't see your mom letting you or your brother stay with me during the winter."

"Nope. Can't see Mom letting Matt and I come in the winter." *I can't see Mom letting you have Matt anytime of the year.*

Rhianna shrugged. She knew better than that. This man was looking for something, but she knew she wasn't going to get him to admit it. "All our back issues are kept in filing cabinets in the basement," she told them. "We were considering having them put on microfilm, the way the big city newspapers do, but so far the guy at the top hasn't decided one way or the other. You'll just have to search through the old copy until you find what you want. You know, I could help if I knew what it is you're really looking for."

Katie had to admire her persistence.

"It's like I told you," Bill said. "Besides, we have nothing better to do on such a muggy day anyway. Right, Kate?" he said with a wink at his daughter.

"Right, Dad." At least it would be cool in the basement, and Katie really didn't want to have to talk to anyone right now.

They followed Rhianna Burke down a thickly carpeted hallway. There were several pictures, and old newspaper photos on the walls. Behind several doors, they could hear the clicking of typewriter keys and voices on telephones. Beside every door, there was a comfortable looking armchair with a stack of magazines. They had certainly tried to keep the cozy warmth of a house, with its thick carpets and comfortable chairs, while utilizing it as an office building with reporters working in every room.

At the end of the hall, Rhianna opened the door, reached in, and pulled the dangling cord. The white glare of the bare bulb made Katie blink. This might not be a dark, dingy basement, but the glare of the bulb did its best to throw grotesque shadows dancing on the walls. Katie couldn't quite suppress a shudder.

"If you're sure you don't require my help, I'll leave you to it. You'll find the files you need at the bottom of the stairs to the left. You shouldn't have any problems. They're all clearly marked. But if you do have any problems, I'll be at my desk." She hesitated, started to walk away, and then turned back. "By the way, if you decide you would like a copy of any of the *events* we have covered, there's a copier just behind the stairs. It's old, but it serves its purpose."

After thanking Rhianna Burke again, they began the long descent to the basement. Bill's look said, "She didn't buy any of it. Did she?" Katie just shrugged.

The light from the single bulb hanging above them didn't quite reach the corners of the cellar. There was, however, enough light to search the files.

The smell of moldy paper, and old chemicals filled Katie's nose. She could hear noises coming from beneath the stairs, and the dark corners of the cellar. Even as she was searching for the dates her father had given her, she tried to keep one eye on those dark places. She didn't want anything pouncing out at her.

"Found it." Katie triumphantly pulled out the file marked September, and walked toward her dad. She didn't see the mouse until it was right in front of her. It stared at her with its beady eyes, then wriggled its nose, and ran back into one of the dark corners. Katie squealed, and threw the file at the mouse. "Look what you've done. You. You. You, rodent, you," she yelled as the newspapers scattered helplessly to the floor.

The mouse had startled Katie, and she tried to cover her reaction with anger. She didn't want her dad to think she was afraid of some silly little mouse. Her dad's quiet laughter filled the small room. She tried to keep her own laughter tamped down, but it bubbled forth as she bent to retrieve the scattered papers.

"Look at this, Dad." She laid the paper out on the floor, and together they read:

WAS IT AN ACCIDENT?

by Loni Roberts

Death is no stranger to our community. Every winter death claims the lives of five or six of our elderly, as if it were its due. Nevertheless, when death claims the life of one of our children, it's always a shock.

It's worse, still, when there is no acceptable reason for such a death. There is no closure for the parents, or the community.

This July a summer resident, Rick Mathers, was the victim of one such accident. Or was he?

The autopsy report clearly showed he was intoxicated. His blood alcohol level was a scandalous.09. Was that enough to send him careening through a railing to his death?

The police seem to think so. "There was a clear indication that the railing was already cracked, causing it to break when the boy, Rick Mathers, lost his balance, and stumbled into it. It has also been found, by the coroner's inquest, that in no way were Mr. and Mrs. Mitchell, the owners of the cabin, in any way negligent." This was a direct quote from our esteemed Police Chief, who doesn't seem in the least bit interested in finding out the truth.

As this reporter sees it, the truth about this boy's death is a mystery yet. True he was drinking. The coroner's evidence and the evidence of his peers proves that. Nevertheless, was his alcohol level such that the boy would lose his balance on a flat surface? If he were going to lose his balance, wouldn't he have done so while climbing the stairs? When he first rose from his seat, wouldn't he have staggered causing him to fall toward the fire? Why wait until he was on a flat surface before staggering to such an extent that he would lose his balance with enough force to break through a protective railing? Of course, the railing was cracked. A slight, hairline crack that wasn't noticeable to the boy or his parents before the accident. Both Mr. and

Mrs. Mathers have testified to this fact.

If you ask me, the evidence does not lead to the conclusion the police have come to. ACCIDENT. Not likely. That is only the opinion of this reporter.

"Be an angel and pick up these papers, Katie. I'm getting a copy of this. Then we're going to the police station."

Fifteen minutes later, they walked in the front door of the police station.

The police station was an almost new, three story building situated next to the fire hall. They entered into a large foyer. The second and third floors had only half walls, and looked out over the open foyer. Green ivy cascaded over these stark white walls with striking contrast.

Several officers passed them by without acknowledging their presence. Katie noticed they were carrying several plastic bags. She could clearly see the large, thick branch in one bag. She shuddered as thoughts of Dave came unbidden. She watched the officers cross the room, their heels silent on the scuffed and gouged hardwood floor, and exit through another door. Nobody in the room seemed to notice them.

Several seconds later, Katie followed her dad across the room. Their own steps seemed incredibly loud on the bare floor. Still nobody took any notice when they passed by several desks, and finally entered the open door at the end of the room. The sign on the door read "Chief Burton."

The officer sitting behind the desk must have heard them enter the room. His floor was as bare as the other one, and their footsteps echoed loudly in Katie's ears. Yet the man didn't raise his head, not even when Katie's dad thumped the copy of the newspaper story on his desk. "I want to talk to you about this story," Bill said.

The Chief of Police, to his credit, calmly picked up the paper, and began to read. He was obviously familiar with the story because he only read a couple of lines before placing the paper back on his desk. His face revealed nothing when he finally raised it. "And who might you be?"

"Bill Davis."

"I see. That explains your obvious interest in this. He half rose, seemed to notice Katie for the first time, and with a flick of his wrist indicated the chairs in front of his desk. "We might as well be comfortable. Have a seat."

He sat back in his own seat, and surveyed the pair in front of him. His eyes missed nothing. Katie was beginning to feel like a specimen in science class, and began to squirm in her seat. The police chief finally broke the silence.

"You must be Katie Williams?" Katie must have looked as startled as she felt. "Officer Black's description was flawless." He rummaged around some papers on his desk, before he picked one up, and began to read. "A quiet, serious young woman, five foot four, approximately seventeen years of age, brown hair, full lips, slightly turned up nose, pale blue eyes, a round, pale face, and a flawless complexion—except for the black circles beneath her eyes." Katie felt her colorless cheeks begin to burn before he finally redirected his attention. "That would make you the father. Do I have it right?"

Bill inclined his head slightly. "And as her father, it is my duty to ensure my daughter's safety."

"Tell me, Mr. Davis. What does this story," he shook the copy slightly. "Have to do with your daughter's safety?"

"Two other boys have died as mysteriously as this boy. They were all staying in the same park we are."

"One drowned. The other was struck on the head by a falling branch during a lightning storm," interrupted the Chief. "Both were unfortunate accidents. I fail to see the connection."

"The same type of accident that befell Rick Mathers?"

"I am not going to discuss this matter with you, Mr. Davis." The police chief rose from his seat, and marched to the open door. "Ralph," he called into the other room. "Show Mr. Davis and his daughter the door. Make sure they leave the building."

Katie scrambled to her feet, while her father rose more slowly. He stopped in front of Chief Burton on his way out, and extended his hand politely. The Chief of Police hesitated almost imperceptibly, and then accepted the outstretched hand. "Thank you for our help, Chief Burton," Bill said, before turning on his heels, and striding out the open door. Katie had to hurry to keep up.

She waited until they were in the car, and on the road to Beechwood, before turning to her father. "What, exactly, was that all about?" she demanded.

"Just a little fishing trip, Katie," he answered with a chuckle.

Katie fumed when he refused to say any more about it. By the time they reached the cabin she was about to erupt. It didn't matter what she did—threaten, plead—he refused to tell her anything that was going on in his mind.

She was so angry she could spit. She was so angry that she didn't notice the other car in the driveway. She got out, and slammed the car door as hard as she could. She jumped when she heard her name. She was so angry she didn't realize it wasn't her father's voice. "What?" she yelled.

"Something wrong, Katie?" She was mortified to find Jack standing beside her. He was going to think her a real shrew. Why was he always around when she lost her temper?

Bill got out of the car, and with a distracted nod in their direction went into the cabin.

"Maybe this isn't a good time," Jack began.

"No. It's fine," she said quickly. She didn't want him to leave. "I thought you were my father. I was waiting for him to give me crap for slamming the car door." She snickered. "I can't believe I actually slammed the door. As if that would bother him. I should know by now that if my father wants to keep a secret nothing in this world will get him to give it up."

"Oh." Jack's interest was piqued, and he glanced at the closed cabin door. "Your father has a secret?"

"Well you don't have to laugh at me," Katie complained. They walked toward the fire pit where Marc was sitting. "It's not like he's hiding something from me. Not really, anyway. It's just that, after I helped him, the least he could do was tell me what he found out. I just don't understand it. We were both sitting there. We both saw and heard the same things. I just can't figure out what he thinks he knows that I don't. And it's driving me crazy."

"What's driving you crazy, Katie?" asked Marc.

"Hey, Marc, how's it going?" Katie grinned at her new friend, determined to put her father, and his little fishing trip, out of her mind.

"I'm good." His eyes flickered to Jack, and back to Katie. "What brings you guys here this early?"

"Don't change the subject," Jack interrupted.

"I wasn't aware we were on a subject."

"Sure we were, Katie," said Jack. "At least you were. You were telling me how you saw and heard everything your father saw and heard, yet you think he knows something that you don't."

"He doesn't know anything," Katie said with a pout. "He just wants me to think he does so I'll be upset."

"Obviously, it's working," Marc stated the obvious. He was having a difficult time keeping a straight face.

"Is not," she insisted. "I know my dad doesn't know anything I don't know."

"Anything?" Jack raised one eyebrow.

Katie blushed, and began to laugh. She was acting like a spoiled child. "Oh, all right," she conceded. "He might know some things I don't know. But not about this."

"And what is this, exactly?" asked Marc, definitely curious now.

"I don't know. That's what's so infuriating."

"Maybe if you told us what you did today, that would help," suggested Jack patiently.

"I don't know, Jack." Katie chewed thoughtfully on her lower lip. It had just occurred to her that Bill might not want anyone to know what he was up to. Not that Katie knew what he was up to, and that was what was so infuriating.

"You don't know what you did?"

"I don't know if it will help to tell you," she hedged.

"Why don't you try?"

Katie looked into his deep penetrating eyes, and was lost. "Okay," she whispered. Katie settled back on a nearby lawn chair, and told them what they had done during the day. She told them about finding the story about Rick at the newspaper office, and then going to the police station. She was preoccupied, trying to figure out what it all meant, and she didn't notice the way Jack's brows were furrowed.

"Well?" she asked when she was finished. "What does my father think he knows?"

Jack glanced at Marc, and shook his head slightly. "Nothing," he finally said. "Your father's obviously teasing you."

"About what?" They all jumped at the sound of Daina's voice. "What is Katie's father teasing her about?" she asked again, and sat in a chair beside Katie.

"The bags under her eyes," Marc said, before anyone else could answer. "He seems to think Katie is carrying around a lot of excess baggage. I don't think it's all that bad. Do you, Jack?"

"No. It's not that bad at all."

Katie was the only one who seemed to notice the angry look Daina gave Marc. "How are you doing, Daina?" she asked. She didn't want Daina and Marc getting into an argument, and for some reason she couldn't fathom, Marc didn't want Daina knowing what they were talking about.

"Better. Well as good as can be expected, anyway."

How well can one expect to be when their friends are dropping like flies? Katie barely knew them, but Jack, Marc, and even Daina had known them for years. They were friends.

The silence around the unlit fire pit was deafening. Katie heard again, the sound of her own voice yelling at Red. Would she ever forget that night? As if her thoughts had conjured him up, Red suddenly took a seat beside Jack. The burning hate in his eyes made Katie shudder. It was hard to tell if he was looking at her or Daina. He spoke directly to Katie.

Help us, he said.

I can't help you. I can't help any of you. You are all dead.

Jack stood up. The sudden movement startled Katie, and she gasped. Red vanished. "I have to go," Jack said. "There's something I have to do."

As if they were in accord, Marc rose at the same time as Jack. Maybe they had a signal they used when things got uncomfortable. "I have to be going too," he said. "But we'll be back later, won't we Jack?"

"Yeah. Later." Distracted, he glanced at the increasing number of clouds. Katie hoped he wasn't going to use the weather as an excuse. "If it's raining, maybe we can play some cards or something."

"Sure," Katie said, her spirits lifted. "We'll play cards, or something."

"Sounds good to me," Daina said. "I haven't played cards in a long time."

Jack nodded in Marc's direction, almost as if he hadn't heard Katie, or Daina. "Come on, then, if you want a lift."

Jack might not have heard them, but Marc had. Katie saw the way he rolled his eyes. He obviously didn't want to spend any more time with Daina than he had to, but Katie felt sorry for Daina. She was hurting, too. "Do you want to walk to the store with me, Daina?" she asked on impulse, after the boys had left. "We can get some chips or something for later."

The look on Daina's face was pitiful. She looked like a little girl who had just gotten her first present from Santa.

Thirteen

THUNDER CONTINUED TO rumble way off in the north. "Do you think it'll rain, Dad?" Katie asked for the twentieth time.

Bill sighed loudly, put his pen down on the table beside him, and leaned back in his chair. He folded his hands in his lap, and studied his daughter. He twirled his thumbs, and watched her fidget. He didn't say a word.

"Well?" she insisted after several agonizing moments of silence. "Do you?"

He made a great show of walking over to the window, and looking out. Katie padded softly behind him, chewing on her bottom lip. Then he went to the front door, and out onto the porch. He looked up into the cloudy sky. Way off in the north the clouds were thick and black. Overhead there were broken patches of grey dispersed with blue.

"I'm not a weatherman," he finally said slowly, and shook his head as he spoke. "But if we do get rain, I'd guess we'd be getting it in the early hours of the morning. In fact, I'd say we're going to get some clear sky and stars tonight."

He squinted, making it look like he was trying to see inside his own head, and sucked on his lower lip. It was something Katie had seen him do many times before, usually when he was concentrating on something important.

"Yes," he finally said. "I do believe things are about to clear up." It didn't sound to Katie as if he were talking about the weather. "Are you planning anything tonight?" he asked suddenly.

"Jack, Marc, and Daina are coming over," she was curious about the slight lift of his eyebrow at the mention of

Daina. "If it rains we were planning on maybe playing cards or something. Is that all right?"

"Sounds like an excellent idea," he said. "In fact I have to go out for awhile myself tonight. I'm glad you won't be alone."

Did he mention going out, and she hadn't been listening? "Where are you going, Dad?"

"It's nothing for you to concern yourself with," he told her, evasively. "Just something I'm working on. I only now remembered that I have to go back to town for awhile." He seemed relieved when Daina appeared on the road. "Hey, Daina," he called cheerfully.

"Hi, Mr. Davis," she called back, waving. "Hey, Katie. Am I the first?"

"Hi, Daina," Katie called back. She knew she had lost her chance to question her father further. She went down to meet Daina, while her father went back into the cabin. There was no sense worrying about what her father was up to. She'd find out when he was ready and not one moment sooner. "The guys aren't here yet."

Daina opened the top of the bag she was carrying, and handed it to Katie. "Look. I brought along a couple of games. In case we don't want to play cards."

Inside the bag were several games. There was Monopoly, Clue, a couple Katie couldn't see the names of, and Twister. "Wow, you have Twister," Katie said. "I thought my mom was the only person in the world who still had that game."

Daina laughed, and her whole face transformed. For the first time since they met, her smile reached her eyes, and she really looked pretty. "I thought it would be fun. I took it from my mom's closet." Daina winked at Katie as if they were conspirators in some great scheme. "I thought maybe we can get the boys to play."

Katie imagined Jack wrapping his arms around her, while he searched for a blue circle. She felt the heat rushing to her cheeks at the image. With a small laugh to hide her wayward thoughts, she grinned at Daina, and said, "This could be a very interesting evening. Come on. Let's put these in the cabin. Do you want a coke or something?"

Mr. Davis was leaving as they were going in. His briefcase was in one hand, his car keys in the other, and he seemed very distracted.

"Bye, Dad," Katie said, and then again louder when he passed them by without answering. "I said, Goodbye, Dad."

He spun around, almost dropping his keys. "Oh! Goodbye, girls." He looked surprised to see them still standing there. "Uh, have fun." Almost as an afterthought, he said. "Don't do anything I wouldn't do." The girls forgotten before he ever reached his car.

Katie put the bag of games on the now empty table, and turned to Daina. "Let's make some popcorn," she said. She was determined to keep her curiosity about her father from ruining her evening.

Kernels pinging steadily against the pot lid when the knock came. Katie was busy shaking the pot, so Daina ran to get the door. She stepped on one of the many little balls of white that littered the floor, and it sounded like squashing a June bug. "Eww. Yuck," she said. Both girls laughed.

When Daina returned, Marc was following her. He was frowning, and pointing his finger at Daina as if to say, "What's she doing here?"

Katie ignored him. He was walking toward the stove when he stepped on a piece of popcorn. The look on his face was hysterical. She burst into laughter.

Daina spun around. Marc was cautiously lifting his foot. He looked as if he expected to find a huge, gooey mess stuck to the bottom of his shoe. Both girls were laughing by the time he realized it was only squashed popcorn.

"Hey. What the...?" Marc began laughing as well, when he notice there was popcorn all over the floor. "How did...?" he began.

Katie lifted the lid, and a few more pieces popped out. "Like that," she said innocently, before removing the pot from the stove. Then, as if she had only now noticed that Marc was alone, she asked. "Where's Jack?"

"I called him before I came up. His aunt said he went some place with his uncle. She didn't know where or when they'd be back."

"Oh." Katie grabbed the broom, and began sweeping up the popcorn, trying to hide the disappointment she was feeling from showing in her voice. "Do you want a coke, Marc?" she asked.

"Sure."

"I'll get it" Daina jumped up, and pulled a can of soda from the fridge. "Glass? Ice?"

"The can's fine," Marc told her, obviously embarrassed by her fussing.

Katie took the dustpan full of popcorn, and tossed it over the back porch. The birds would eat the corn in the morning. "Guess what, Marc?" she said when she returned to the kitchen. "Daina brought Twister." She put the broom and dustpan away, all the time surreptitiously watching Marc. She could see the thoughts rolling around behind his eyes. *I'll get you for this*, they seemed to say. Katie relented. She knew Daina had a crush on Marc, but it was just as obvious that Marc didn't feel the same way. "It's too bad Jack isn't here. It's no good playing Twister with only three. One has to call the colors, and you need at least three playing to make it interesting."

The relief on Marc's face was as comical as the disappointed on Daina's was painful. No one suggested lighting the fire, and so they settled down to play games. After a slightly heated discussion, Daina wanted to play Clue, Katie opted for Risk, and Marc wanted to play Monopoly, they decided to solve the debate by drawing straws. Marc won.

Now Katie landed on Boardwalk for the third time in a row. Every time she landed on it, Marc used the rent she paid to add more dwellings, thus increasing the rent for the next time. He was now up to hotels, and was rubbing his hands together gleefully in anticipation of the money he was about to rake in.

Katie looked at her meager pile of bills, and knew she didn't have enough to pay, and with her properties already mortgaged, there was no chance of a loan from the bank. Maybe she could get a loan from Daina. A quick glance in that direction showed her Daina's properties were mortgaged as well.

She threw her hands in the air in mock surrender. "Okay, take my money, and quit gloating," she said with a laugh. "At least you can't have my properties. They go back to the bank."

Marc calmly sorted her bills in with his own. "Who wants them, anyway," he teased, unperturbed. "They're not worth anything. They're mortgaged to the hilt."

"Get lost," Katie retorted with a giggle. "You know you want them. But you ain't gonna get them. Daina's going to land on them, and buy them all up. Then she's going to beat you at your own game. Aren't you, Daina?"

"I would. Except I have to be home by the time the restaurant closes at eleven. And it's quarter to now."

"Well, then. We'll walk you home. Won't we, Marc?"

"Of course we will. Can't let a lady walk through those dark, creepy woods alone," he said gallantly.

Daina blushed enchantingly. "Why thank you, kind sir," she returned in kind.

They gathered the games together, and headed down the road. The thunder was long gone, and it had turned into a beautiful night. The sky had cleared, and several stars were twinkling above. Daina walked so close to Marc that she literally tripped him several times. He rolled his eyes at Katie over Daina's head, but said nothing to Daina.

When they arrived at Daina's house, Marc quickly handed her the bag of games. "We'll wait right here until you are safely inside," he told her.

Daina had no choice except to go up the stairs. Katie couldn't help notice the way Daina was beaming with happiness when they said their goodbyes, but the moment the door shut behind her, Marc grabbed Katie's hand, and pulled her toward the road. "Whew. I'm glad that's over," he said in a stage whisper.

"What's the matter, Marc?" teased Katie. "Were you afraid she was going to jump you right there in the woods?"

Marc feigned horror at the thought. They were both still laughing and holding hands when they headed back toward the cabin. Neither noticed Daina watching from her window. If they had, they would have had cause for alarm. The hatred in her face was plain even from that distance. As it was, they cheerfully went on their way, laughing and talking.

Her dad still wasn't home when they returned, and neither one wanted to go indoors yet. They decided to sit on the back porch for a while.

It became a magical place. The stars waltzed like fairies across the water to the music of the tree toads. Marc pointed out the large and small dippers. "On a clear night, you can see the Milky Way," he told her. Katie relaxed as he began a dialogue about the different constellations.

Finally, around midnight Katie couldn't suppress her yawns anymore, and Marc left.

Fourteen

HELP US, KATIE.

Katie opened her eyes, and glared at the three boys standing at the side of her bed. "Go away," she hissed.

Help us, Katie.

"Walk into the light," she suggested sarcastically.

Come on, Katie. This is important. Dave reached down to shake Katie's shoulder, and Katie shivered when his hand slid through her flesh like an icy knife. She might see and hear ghosts, but this was the first time she felt one, and it was not a good feeling.

Katie sighed, and sat up, rubbing the grit from her eyes. She couldn't remember the last time she had a good night's sleep. Was it only a week ago? That couldn't be right. It must be longer than that.

Now that they had her attention, the three boys moved back from the bed to give her space. The chill emanating from their combined forms was invading the room, and she was thankful for their consideration. She pulled the comforter in front of her as a shield against the cold.

Red claimed the chair at the bottom of the bed, while Dave perched on the edge of the desk by the window. Rick glided across the floor to the window. Now that they had her attention, he seemed to be ignoring her to scan the woods outside the window. They were paler, but other than that they looked like they had when they were alive, a good thing since she was having a hard enough time getting the image of Shaun's bloated face from imposing itself over this paler image. His eyes were red-rimmed, and Katie wondered if he had been crying. She couldn't blame him if he had. She'd cry too if she were dead.

"I'm sorry, Shaun," she whispered.

Shaun's image shrugged. *Don't worry about it, Katie. It wasn't your fault.*

Although she could see his lips move, Katie heard the words in her head instead of her ears. "I shouldn't have lost my temper."

Aw, Katie. Jack was right. I was drunk, and I was being a jerk. He winked. *You can't blame a guy for trying.*

Shut up, Shaun. We don't have time for this.

Katie's eyes flew to Rick. He was staring out the window, and she could tell he was extremely agitated. He suddenly spun around to face her.

Help us, his eyes begged.

Katie ran her fingers through her hair, and gripped the back of her head in frustration. *I can't help you,* she thought. *You're dead.*

Yes. Dave said his tone somber. *But Marc isn't.*

Fifteen

KATIE CAME AWAKE INSTANTLY.

Not Marc.

She sat up, rubbing the sleep from her eyes. She was still trying to make sense of her dream when she heard anxious voices in the other room. Here we go again. Quickly she pulled on jeans and a yellow sweatshirt, and went to join her dad in the hallway. He was with Daina and a man Katie had never seen before—although his eyes were familiar. Daina's face was blotchy, and her eyes red rimmed. That brought back the image of Shaun and the visit the night before.

"Katie," her dad said. "This is Mr. Randall. Marc's father."

Katie was too stunned to respond. Her heart landed in the pit of her stomach with a thud. The blood drained from her face. *Not Marc too*, she cried silently. *It was just a nightmare. Please don't let it be too late for Marc.* She was so lost in her own thoughts she almost missed Daina's triumphant words.

"Katie will know where Marc is Mr. Randall."

"Hush, Daina." Mr. Randall spoke kindly, yet firmly. "Katie," he said in that same kind voice. "I hate to have to ask, but when was the last time you saw my son, Marc?"

"Last night. As Daina has probably already told you, we walked her home about eleven. Then we came back here and sat on the back porch for a while, and talked. He left about midnight."

"What did you talk about?"

"Mostly the stars. Marc knows a lot about the constellations. He was explaining them to me."

"Where was he going when he left here?" asked Mr. Randall.

"Home. At least I thought that's where he was going. He didn't actually say where he was going."

"But he didn't go home. Did he, Katie?" Daina sounded so positive it made Katie wonder what she knew.

"Why don't you tell me, Daina? If Marc didn't go home, where did he go?"

It was Daina's turn to look flustered. "Don't try to make this about me," she said angrily. "I wasn't the last person to see Marc alive."

"Girls." Mr. Davis spoke for the first time since introducing Marc's father. "This is not helping anyone."

"Well it's true," Daina said with a whine. "She was the last person to see Marc. She was the last person to see Shaun, and she was the last person to see Dave. Why don't you ask her what happened to them?" She was almost hysterical now. "Ask her what's happening to everybody since she came here."

Katie was speechless. They had such a good time last night. How could Daina possibly think she had anything to do with the accidents? Besides, nobody even knew what, if anything had happened to Marc.

A memory was tugging at her. What was it Dave said? *Marc isn't.* Isn't what? Dead? It had to be true. Marc was alive, besides, he hadn't come back last night so that was a good sign.

Mr. Randall snapped at Daina. "Stop that immediately. No one knows that anything has happened to Marc, and nobody is accusing this child of any wrong doing. As far as we know, Marc may have gone off with Jack somewhere. It wouldn't be the first time. In fact, I should have thought of that before I allowed you to bring me here."

Daina adopted a shamefaced expression. "You're absolutely right, Mr. Randall. I am over reacting, and I'm sorry. I'm sorry too, Mr. Davis. I shouldn't have jumped to conclusions."

She said nothing to Katie, but her eyes spoke volumes. "You are responsible for everything that is happening around here," they said. Katie suppressed a shudder, and said nothing.

"I'm sorry for disturbing you, Mr. Davis. Katie." Mr. Randall turned to Daina. "Come along, Daina. It's time to call Jack. If he hasn't heard from Marc then I'll call the police and arrange for a search party. That's what I should have done in the first place, instead of bothering these people, and wasting precious time."

"Are you going to be all right, Katie?" asked her dad. Katie nodded. "Good." He followed Mr. Randall and Daina down the front steps. "If you don't mind, Mr. Randall. I'd like to come with you. If Jack hasn't heard from Marc I'd like to help with the search."

Katie made herself a sandwich she didn't really want, and looked at the clock. One o'clock. Still no sign of Marc or her dad. Katie took her sandwich out to the front porch. She would eat it out there. That way she would know the moment her father returned.

After taking only two bites, she put the unfinished sandwich back on the plate, and shoved it aside. It was no use. She wasn't going to be able to eat anything until she knew what was going on. Where was everyone? Had they found Marc? Was he all right? Was he off with Jack somewhere?

The questions ran through her mind with nothing to stop them. She had no answers. Nothing concrete to go on. Yet she was convinced Marc was alive, but if he was, why hadn't they found him yet?

A snapping branch brought her back to reality. There were several kids gathered in front of the cabin now. Daina was with them. They weren't close enough for her to hear what they said, but she knew they were talking about her. It was hard not to know. They kept pointing at her then putting their heads together. What else could they be talking about? It wasn't long before her worst fears were confirmed.

"Who's next?" someone shouted. "Do you have a list?"

Katie was beginning to get angry. What were they accusing her of? She hadn't done anything. "Why are you doing this to me?" she screamed at them. "What have I ever done to you?"

"Nothing yet," came the quick reply. "But then, who knows?"

"What about Shaun?" a voice cried. "You know what she did to Shaun?"

"And Dave," a different voice echoed.

"Where's Marc?" Daina asked. "Why don't you tell us what you did with Marc?"

The others repeated the question like a chant. "Where's Marc? Where's Marc?" they repeated repeatedly.

"Stop it," Katie screamed. "Stop it, or..."

"Or what?" Daina stepped to the front of the crowd. "Are you going to curse us like you did the others?"

"I don't know what you're talking about," insisted Katie. "Why are you doing this, Daina?"

"Me." Daina laughed viciously. "Why do you always insist on trying to turn this on me? Everyone here knows I'm not the one who sent Shaun and Dave to their deaths."

"What are you trying to say?" demanded Katie nearly choking on her fury.

"Get off it, Katie. Everyone knows you're responsible. What was it you said to Shaun? 'Eat dirt and die,' I think were you're exact words. What happened? He went down to the beach and choked on a mouthful of dirt."

"I never," Katie began again, only to be interrupted yet again.

"But you did. Didn't you?"

"NO," she answered more emphatically.

"Yes you did." Daina repeated herself as she would if she were talking to a small child. "Don't you remember? Then, when you were through with Shaun, you turned to Dave. What was it you told him? Oh yeah. 'Don't go out into the storm,' you warned him. 'You might get hurt.' And he did, didn't he? Just like you said he would." Daina's voice became sweeter with every word she spoke.

"It was the storm," Katie tried to tell them. "I didn't do anything."

"Of course you did, Katie. Don't you remember? You pretended to warn Dave when all the time you were calling on the forces of nature to do your bidding." Suddenly her face filled with understanding. "That's it. Isn't it? You're a witch."

"I am not." Katie tried again to convince them.

"Then last night you turned on Marc. I heard you myself," Daina continued, not in the least interested in Katie's denials. "You told Marc to get lost. And now he is. Where did you send him, Katie? Why don't you just tell us?"

"It was a joke. We were playing a game. You were there, Daina. You know what happened."

Her smile was truly evil. "I was, wasn't I," she said.

Katie turned, and ran into the cabin. She locked the door behind her, but she couldn't lock out the sound of their voices.

Sixteen

SHE DIDN'T HEAR his car arrive. Neither did the others, and they were outside. It didn't take Mr. Davis long to make his presence known.

"WHAT'S GOING ON?" he demanded.

They scattered. Like rats fleeing the proverbial sinking ship, they disappeared into the woods. Katie watched from her new perch behind the curtain, but it didn't matter anymore. Sure, they were gone now, but they would return. Of that, she was certain.

She remained behind the curtain, peeking out into the now empty yard, even after her father came up the stairs, and crossed the porch. He found his daughter behind the curtain, after he had to go back to the car to get his key so he could unlock the door.

"They're gone," he said simply.

"For how long? Five minutes? Ten? Tomorrow?"

"I don't know."

"Did you find Marc?" She already knew the answer. Still, stubborn hope made her ask.

"No. Mr. Randall phoned Jack, but he hadn't heard from him. I think every father, and several mothers, helped to search the entire park, and most of the surrounding area. There was no sign of him. The police are taking over the search.

Katie finally left the window, and sat on one of the couches. She pulled her feet up, and wrapped her arms around her knees. She made herself as small as she could, and tried to escape reality. "They blame me, you know. Who's to say they're not right. Maybe I'm just bad luck."

"That's ridiculous and you know it."

"Maybe I do. Maybe I don't. It doesn't really matter anymore. I've made up my mind. I want to go home."

"Why? Are you afraid?"

"Yes I'm afraid." Katie heard the hysteria rising in her voice, and forced herself to remain calm. "Face it, Dad. People are either dying, or disappearing. First Shaun. Then Dave. Now Marc. Who's next? Jack? Daina? Me?" Although, something told her that Daina alone was not in any real danger. "I can't stand it anymore. Everyone I even remotely get close to. Why is that? Can you explain it? Because I can't. I can't explain anything that has happened since I first came to this place."

"I'll figure it out, Katie. I promise. I just need a little more time."

"It's too late, Dad. I don't have any more time. I want to leave. Now. Today."

"Okay. If you want to go, we'll go."

He gave in much too easily. Katie knew it, but she didn't stop to dwell on it. "Fine." She said as she headed for her room. "I'm going to pack."

Less than ten minutes later Katie had completed her ramshackle packing. With her knapsack hanging off one shoulder, and her suitcase clutched in hand, she threw open the door—and froze.

"Going somewhere, Miss Williams?" asked Officer Black, brusquely.

Katie let her suitcase fall with a thud, and shrugged her pack off her shoulder. "No," she said. "I'm not going anywhere." She stepped back to allow the officer entry.

"Come in, Officer Black. Can I get you a cup of tea?" He looked like he could use something much stronger than tea. His uniform was rumpled, his shoes caked in dried mud, and he looked like he hadn't slept in a week, which is how Katie felt. "You'll be more comfortable in the living room I think. I'll just go get Dad."

She rapped on her father's door, opened it, and walked in without waiting for a reply. "What's this?" she asked. He was sitting in the middle of his bed with papers strewn all around him. He hadn't started to pack. Worse, he wasn't in the least bit embarrassed that she found out. "Officer Black is in the living room," she finally said. She knew he wasn't going to say anything.

Her dad nonchalantly glanced at his watch, and then rose slowly from his bed, being careful not to disturb the papers there. "I thought they would have sent someone sooner," he said. "You better join us, Katie. I'm almost positive that Officer Black will want to ask you some questions."

Of course, he wanted to ask her questions. Katie went to the kitchen to make the tea. She wasn't looking forward to talking to Officer Black. In fact, she didn't want to talk to him at all, and making tea was an excuse not to join them right away.

She took her time. First, she found an old tin cookie tray in the drawer beneath the stove. She took her time arranging the teapot, and three cups on the tray, before she added honey and lemon. Then she added sugar and a small cup of milk— Officer Black might not want honey or lemon—then she added a few cookies. After rearranging the tray several times, she finally admitted to herself that she couldn't put off talking to the officer any longer.

She picked up the tray, straightened her shoulders and headed for the living room, but stopped at the kitchen door. Her father and the police officer were walking towards the front door, and she could hear them talking.

"No problem, Officer," her dad was saying.

"I'm glad you understand, Sir. I just hope your daughter will be as understanding when she finds out she can't leave yet."

"Don't worry about Katie. She'll be just fine."

Katie replaced the tray on the counter, and sat at the table. She would take her things back to her room after the officer was gone.

Seventeen

WHEN KATIE'S FATHER came back in the house five minutes later he wasn't alone.

"How are you doing, Katie?" asked Jack.

Her disappointment at not being able to go home disappeared, and she smiled at Jack. He was the one bright spot in this whole mess. "A lot better now," she told him cheerfully. "How about you?"

"Holding on." He pulled out a chair, and sat across from her. "Mind if I join you?"

Mind. Of course she didn't mind. "Do you think it's safe?" she teased, as her father excused himself to go to his room. "Being alone with me, I mean."

Jack ignored her comment. "Your dad told me what happened earlier. You can't let it get to you, Katie. Nobody believes you had anything to do with Marc's disappearance."

"Then why won't the police let me leave? And it's not just Marc," she added. "It's Shaun and Dave too. Daina is telling everyone that will listen that I'm responsible for their deaths. And if nobody believes her then why can't I go home?" She knew she sounded peevish but she couldn't help it. "Forget it," she said before Jack had a chance to answer. "What about Marc? Have you heard anything?" she added quickly.

"Nothing yet."

"What do you really think happened to him?" She asked. She didn't want to ask, but she had to find out for herself if Jack really blamed her. The only way to find out was to ask the question. She would know if he was lying.

"I don't know. I know he didn't just wander off somewhere without telling his folks. And I know you didn't lure him off somewhere," he added quickly. Katie's spirits rose a good ten degrees. Jack didn't blame her at all. "Sure, we used to take off sometimes on the spur of the moment," he continued, completely unaware of the test he'd just passed. "But we'd always call our folks from wherever we landed. There's no way Marc would take off by himself, and let his mother worry like this. Not with everything else that's happened around here lately. It's just not like him."

He was right. Marc didn't just wander off somewhere. He was lured away, and he wasn't staying away willingly. Katie wanted to tell Jack about the feelings she got, but she was afraid. Would he believe her? Would he think her crazy? She started talking quickly, before she could change her mind. "Do you believe that what happened to Shaun and Dave were simply accidents?"

"The evidence seems to point in that direction." He might have said the words, but his tone wasn't very convincing.

"That's what I'm talking about," Katie spoke quickly with excitement. "They seem to be accidents. That doesn't mean they were."

"What are you trying to say, Katie?"

"What if Shaun's drowning wasn't an accident? What if someone killed him?"

"Why would someone kill Shaun?"

"I don't know. I don't believe for one minute that his drowning was an accident. The more I think about it, the more I'm convinced." After a few moments without Jack saying anything, she continued. "I keep going over the scene in my mind. I remember thinking it was strange the way Shaun's foot was caught in the rope of the boat."

"What do you mean, caught?" asked Jack, suddenly very interested.

"I was thinking. If he had been jogging along the beach and tripped over the rope, wouldn't his foot be in front of the rope on the ground? Or even draped over the top of it, by the ankle?"

"It was on the ground."

"Why do you say that?" asked Katie.

"I remember reading it in the report."

"But that's not right. When I found Shaun, his foot was tangled in the boat rope. I had to unwind it at least twice to get his foot free so I could turn him over. I remember that every time I tried to turn him so his face wasn't in the water, he rolled back."

"Did you tell the police this?"

"Of course." Katie went over the scene in her mind again. *She found Shaun's body. She tried to turn him over so his face wasn't in the water, but he kept turning back, as if something were holding him face down. That's when she noticed the rope wrapped around his foot. Then there was a blank until she was back at the cabin with Daina.* "Maybe not," she admitted. She couldn't figure out how the rope wrapped around his ankle. "I really can't remember what happened from the time I found Shaun until Daina and I got back here."

"Is it possible, do you think?" Jack asked. "Could you have tangled Shaun's foot while you were trying to turn him over?" When Katie glared at him, he quickly continued. "Just think about it for a moment, will you. You can't go around accusing someone of doing something without proof. That's as bad as Daina accusing you."

"Your right, of course. It's not just his foot. It's everything."

"What do you mean everything? What else is there?"

Well, it's now or never. If she didn't tell him about her feelings soon, she never would. "This is going to sound crazy, but I had a dream about the night Rick died."

"I don't doubt it. Especially after everything that's happened around here."

"You don't get it. I had the dream before I knew about Rick. It was while I was in the car on the way here. Then the day we arrived, I got a strange feeling when I was standing on the deck. I get them sometimes. It's as if I know what happened, without really knowing. Do you know what I mean?" She didn't tell him about the ghosts, after all, there was no reason for him to think she was insane.

Katie looked up, and met Jack's penetrating brown eyes. She shivered slightly, but not from cold. "Why don't you explain what you mean?" he said.

Great, she thought. He thinks I'm crazy. "It's like, sometimes I know that something has happened but I don't know what," she tried to explain. "Or sometimes, I know someone has done something but I can't be sure what they did or why. I can usually tell when someone is lying. Then there are the dreams. I see things in my dreams. Things that happen. Sometimes they are about to happen. But more often they've already happened."

"And you saw Rick die in a dream," Jack interrupted suddenly understanding. "Tell me exactly what you saw, Katie."

"I was standing at the top of the steps. The ones leading to the back deck. Only I didn't know that they were the steps until later. Anyway, there was a boy leaning against the railing. It looked like he was nearly asleep. He couldn't have been because he suddenly stood up, and turned to face the house. I turned to see what he was looking at. There was nothing there except shadows." Katie couldn't help but shudder at the memory of those shadows.

"Then the strangest thing happened. A section of the shadows separated from the others. It began to look almost human, and it was moving towards the boy. Suddenly, without really knowing why, I was terrified. I tried to call out a warning to the boy. He was leaning against the railing again, and couldn't hear me. The louder I tried to yell, the quieter my own voice got. The shadow kept moving closer and closer, and I could feel the terror building. I tried to run to the boy. I knew I had to warn him the shadows were coming. It felt like my feet were glued to that step. I couldn't move. The shadows kept getting closer and closer, until finally the shadow came right up behind him, and pushed him through the railing." Katie stopped talking, and looked at Jack. His reaction surprised her. He seemed excited.

"I've got to go," he said as he rose quickly from his chair. "Don't tell anyone else about this, okay? I'll be back later." Katie stared at Jack, her confusion obvious. "Promise me," Jack insisted. "Don't talk to anyone."

Katie promised, and walked Jack out. They had no sooner stepped onto the porch than the taunts began once more. Her father's window faced this side of the house. He must have heard the voices because within seconds he stuck his head out the window, and ordered Katie's tormentors to leave. Some fled. Most stood their ground.

"Why don't you just go home?" Katie felt as if they'd kicked her in the stomach. Why couldn't they leave her alone? "Go home," they began chanting.

"If I were you," Jack addressed the crowd. "I'd take my own advice, and go home," with emphasis on the last two words. "Leave Katie alone."

Katie's dad remained in the window, but he seemed more interested in seeing how Jack was going to handle the crowd than doing anything himself.

"If you knew the truth, Jack, you wouldn't defend her." Daina moved to the front of the crowd, and glared. Katie shouldn't have been surprised. For some reason, and only Daina knew what that reason was, she had it in for Katie.

"Why don't you tell me the truth, Daina," Jack said.

"She's a murderer. Everyone knows it. Even the police."

"Is that so?" Jack stepped off the stairs, and faced Daina, his dark eyes furious. Not once did he raise his voice above a conversational tone, and it was doubtful that those hanging back could hear. "If she is a murderer, why hasn't she been arrested? If the police know for a fact that she is a murderer why are they letting her run around, free to murder again?"

Daina seethed. Her face was livid, her eyes bugged out, and she began to gasp in rage. "You better watch yourself, Jack," she bit out viciously. "You might be next."

On that note, Daina turned, and stalked down the road. Her faithful followers right behind.

Eighteen

KATIE TOOK HER cases to her room and unpacked. As she put her last sweater in a drawer, her stomach growled. She headed for her father's room, and rapped on the door. This time she waited for a response.

"Come in, Katie," he said.

She found him sitting exactly the way she had when Officer Black had arrived, on his bed surrounded by papers. He looked up when she entered. "What's up?"

"I'm hungry," she told him bluntly, rubbing her stomach to emphasize the remark. "The only thing I've eaten today was a bit of sandwich around one o'clock. Aren't you getting hungry? Do you want me to make some supper?"

Her dad dropped his pencil on a pile of papers, and jumped off the bed. "To tell the truth, Katie, I don't feel much like hot dogs. Let's go down to the restaurant, and get a real home cooked meal."

Katie recoiled as if he'd hit her. It was bad enough they had to stay here in the cabin, he couldn't possibly expect her to eat in that busy restaurant where everyone would be staring at her. "I'm just going to grab a sandwich," she said, turning to leave the room.

"Hold on, Katie. You have to eat, and I want to go out."

"Then go out," she told him peevishly. "I'm going to stay right here and have a sandwich."

"No you're not," her dad insisted. "You are going to get cleaned up, and then you are coming to the restaurant with your father. You have done nothing wrong, and it's about time you stopped hiding inside this cabin like a criminal."

Katie couldn't believe what her father was saying. "I'm not hiding," she protested.

"Then how come you're not down at the beach swimming, out playing basketball, or volleyball? Face it, Katie. You're hiding. Besides, I need to make a few phone calls, and I want to find out if there's any news."

Katie wasn't a stupid girl, and she knew when she was beat. "I get the shower first," she said in way of concession.

"Fine. But save some hot water for me," her dad called after her retreating back.

The sharp sting of the cold spray did a lot towards washing away Katie's black mood. It looked like her dad wasn't getting hot water after all. She had to admit her father was right—as usual. She'd done nothing wrong, and it was about time she quit acting as if she had. As long as she was stuck here, she was going to spend her time more productively. After all, she was on vacation.

As luck would have it, the restaurant was the busiest Katie had seen. Both small rooms were packed, and there was no room at the counter. Katie shrugged her shoulders, tried to suppress the glee she felt at this development, and turned to her dad. "Do you want to drive to town?" she asked hopefully.

"I'll get us a couple of menus," he told her. "We can order something to go."

Unfortunately, before they had a chance to place their orders, the server told them a small table in the corner was available.

The minute Katie walked into the room she felt every eye turn her way. The room, which was previously a buzz of conversation, suddenly became as quiet as a tomb. Katie just knew they had been talking about her. Her dad managed to ignore everyone in the room except the server, and walked straight to the table she motioned them to. He placed his hand on the small of Katie's back, forcing her to walk ahead of him.

To make matters worse, when she pulled her chair out from under the table, a leg caught on the carpet, and the chair crashed noisily to the floor. Katie clamped her teeth down to keep from screaming aloud, and righted the chair as if nothing had happened. Then she plunked herself down on the seat, and hid her face behind her menu. The conversation around them picked up again, this time as mere whispers, further convincing Katie that she was the topic of conversation. Or rather more specifically, what they believed that she had done to Shaun, Dave, and Marc.

Katie slammed her menu down on the table, and raged inwardly. She had to get herself under control. If she kept on like this, she was going to start to believe Daina's crazy accusations herself. Good manners forced Katie to smile politely at the server, when she placed their water and silverware on the table before them.

The server was just a few years older than Katie. She had sandy colored hair, which she wore in a long braid that hung down her back, and sparkling blue eyes. She was wearing blue jeans and an oversized white t-shirt with a cartoon of a fish in a boat. The fish was fishing for a swimmer using a mermaid for bait. However, the girl's smile stood out the most. It was genuine and friendly.

Katie found herself smiling back with more warmth than she originally used. For a few moments, anyway, she was able to ignore the other diners, and relax.

"Have you decided what you'd like?" the server asked. As she spoke, she was busy putting ketchup, and other condiments on the table. "Our special today is the roast beef dinner." She wrinkled her nose at Katie. "I know for a fact that it's delicious. I can also recommend the camp burger platter. Most of the teenagers prefer it. It's a homemade beef burger with bacon and cheese on a fresh baked Kaiser, and served with golden brown fries and coleslaw. Gravy is optional."

The girl laughed quietly, and several heads turned their way. "Listen to me," she said humor still evident in her voice. "I sound like a commercial. The next thing you know, I'll be singing jingles."

With all eyes once again facing her way, Katie squirmed. Both Katie and her dad ordered the roast beef with mashed potatoes and gravy. Katie opted for the mixed vegetables, while her dad settled for the coleslaw. They both ordered iced tea, which the server brought immediately. Then the moment their server left the room to place their food order, the whispering continued.

"I can't believe that they're acting like nothing has happened," they heard someone from another table say.

Katie made a concentrated effort to ignore the other diners, and enjoy her father's company. "So, what have you been working on, Dad?" she asked, a forced smile plastered on her pale face. She wasn't going to let rumors spoil her dinner, even if it killed her.

"Have you read anything about the Columbian drug lords?" Katie nodded, her eyes wide with interest. "Well, I'm not doing a story on them," he quipped.

"Dad!" Katie threw her napkin across the table at him. He ducked in mock fear of the projectile, even though the napkin barely made it to his side of the table.

"Seriously," he told her. He picked up the napkin, and carefully folded it, before he placed it beside her plate. "You know I never talk about my work until it's finished."

Katie knew it was true. That's just one of many things her parents would argue about, his continual secrets. "Sorry."

"There is something I want to talk to you about, though," he said.

Their server chose that moment to arrive with their meal. They thanked her, and as she was leaving Katie's dad called her back. "Is there a phone around here I could use?" he asked. He had finally given up trying to get a signal with his cell phone.

"I'm sure Mrs. Mitchell will let you use the one in her office, Mr. Davis." Katie wasn't surprised that the girl knew who her father was. She was surprised that he asked about a phone. After all, he had already used Mrs. Mitchell's phone several times.

"I was thinking more along the lines of a public telephone."

"Oh. There's one outside. When you leave the restaurant, turn right and go around back. It's beneath the stairs leading to the Mitchell's apartment."

Katie didn't remember seeing a phone the night she and Marc walked Daina home. But then again, she wasn't really looking for a phone. "I don't remember seeing a phone there," she mentioned.

"That's not surprising," the server said. "It's pretty well hidden beneath the stairs, and the sign's been knocked down so many times that the Mitchell's just gave up putting it back. Almost everyone around here knows it's there, so it's no big deal."

Before he'd even finished his dinner, Katie's dad excused himself to make a phone call. When he came back to the table, he was very distracted. "Are you going to eat all that?" he asked before she had finished her meal.

Katie put her fork down, and pushed her plate away. She had seen her father like this before. He had a lead, and he was anxious to follow up on it. "I'm finished," she said. "I wasn't very hungry anyway."

"Good." He rose from the table, and ignoring the curious looks of the other diners, went to pay his bill.

Katie quickly followed. "What's going on, Dad?" she asked as soon as they left the restaurant.

"I was just talking to Officer Black."

"What were you talking to him for?" Katie couldn't keep the nervous tremor out of her voice.

"I wanted to know if they'd found Marc yet. And I had a few questions to ask."

"Does this have anything to do with why they won't let me leave?"

"Yes it does. Listen, Katie. I can't say anything about it right now, but I have to go out for a while."

"Out? You're going to go out, and leave me here?" She couldn't believe her ears. Teenagers were disappearing, and worse, and he wanted to leave her alone. Forget that almost everyone thought she had something to do with it.

"I won't be gone long. What I need you to do is stay in the cabin. Keep the doors locked, and don't talk to anyone."

"You're kidding, right? This is some kind of joke." Her voice broke slightly. "If it wasn't safe you wouldn't leave me alone. Would you?"

"Don't be ridiculous, Katie. As long as you do what I say, you'll be perfectly fine. I'll try to be back early, but I can't guarantee it. I need to know you're safe."

"Of course I'll be safe."

Nineteen

"DID YOU GET THEM?" Katie pulled Jack through the open door, and then quickly looked around to make sure nobody was watching, before she slammed and locked the door.

Jack sauntered toward the kitchen, a mischievous twinkle in his eye, and a grin on his smug face. He waggled his dark eyebrows mischievously. "We're alone at last."

Heat stole into her cheeks turning them crimson, and her eyes darted frantically around the room, searching for something to say.

Jack chuckled. "In that case, do you have anything to drink? Or should I run back to the store?"

"Jack!" She couldn't hide the frustration in her voice. The man ran hot and cold, then again, she hadn't exactly had anything fitting to say.

"Come on, Katie," he wheedled. "I've been busy ever since I got your call. You can't begrudge me a drink, can you?"

Katie was suitably chastised. She was the one who had enlisted Jack's help. Besides, she had already waited for two hours for him to get here, what was a couple more minutes. "Will a soda do?" she asked. "Or would you rather I made tea?" She hoped he'd settle for soda. It was quicker.

Jack dropped the envelope he was carrying on the table. "A soda would be great." He pulled out a chair, and dropped into it. "To tell the truth, I'm not fussy on tea. I don't know how you and your father can drink so much of it. Thanks," he said when she handed him his drink. "When did you say your dad was coming back?"

Katie pulled a chair beside Jack, and sat down. "Later," she answered evasively. Her father's final warning was still ringing in her ears. "Shaun's death was no accident," he told her. "Someone killed him, and that someone is still out there. Keep the doors locked, and don't let anyone in." Katie hoped that didn't include Jack. She had snuck down to the phone under the stairs, and called Jack as soon as her father left.

Katie couldn't stand the suspense any longer. "Is the report in here?" she asked, reaching for the envelope.

"No. That's my baby pictures."

"Don't tease, Jack," Katie rebuked. She tore the envelope open, and emptied the contents on the table in front of her. There were a lot more papers than she'd expected. There was something familiar about them. She picked up the nearest page and looked at the official seal, her head cocked to one side, thinking. It wasn't until she'd dropped the page back on the table that it hit her. "I've seen these before," she blurted out. "On Dad's bed."

"Are you sure?"

"I'm not positive. But, yeah, I'm sure."

Jack's laugh was low and warm, like his voice. "I'm glad you're sure," was all he said.

"When Officer Black came earlier, Dad was sitting on his bed surrounded by papers," she continued, unperturbed. "I didn't think too much of it. It's a scene I've seen a thousand times. Some papers were hand written notes, the kind he always writes to himself when he's working. Others were neatly typed. Then later, after you left and I finished unpacking, I went to see if he was hungry. Dad was reading, and when I went in, he dropped the page. That was when I saw the seal." She tapped the page in front of her. "It was this same seal."

"That doesn't mean he had a copy of these reports. All autopsy reports done at Lindsay Medical Centre have the same seal. He could have been working on something completely unrelated."

Jack had a point. "You're probably right," she conceded. Katie picked up the page and began reading.

Autopsy Report

Lindsay Medical Centre

Katie quickly scanned past the date, address, and phone number, and then began to read.

The following is a summary of the autopsy performed on one Richard Mathers; male; approximately 17 years of age; performed by Dr. Franklin Schwartz.

Katie skimmed over what she considered irrelevant information, and began reading again:

Blood Alcohol .09

Then further. "Here it is," she said excitedly.

> There were several superficial cuts and bruises consistent with a fall from a high deck. Some internal bruising. The cartilage in the right kneecap was torn. The left tibia fractured in three places. The spinal cord torn between the first and second vertebrae.
>
> Cause of death: broken neck.

Then Jack handed Katie the police report, pointing to the significant line. It read: "Death by misadventure."

"What does it mean?" she asked.

Jack took a drink, and then exchanged his soda for the autopsy report. He pretended to read it, despite the fact that he could have recited it verbatim with his eyes closed. He had read, and re-read, the original at least a hundred times since the accident happened. However, this was the first time he had a reasonable explanation for the internal bruise.

"When I left here earlier, I went straight to the files room and pulled this report. There has always been something that didn't seem right about it. Then, when you were telling your story this afternoon, it hit me. The bruise." He shook the paper violently. It was the first time Katie had ever seen him so upset. "Nobody could explain this bruise to my satisfaction. Until now."

Katie wiggled around until she was more comfortable. "Explain it to me."

"I called Dr. Schwartz in Lindsay. That's what took me so long. I was waiting for him to return my calls. Anyway, when I asked him last year about the bruise, he had no explanation. Then today I gave him your scenario, and he confirmed that it was possible that that was how the bruise occurred. Not from running into an object, but from adding to pressure that was already there."

"What about the others?" Katie asked. "Have you read the other reports?"

Jack searched through the papers on the table, eventually withdrawing two from the pile. He handed Katie one. "Read this first," he told her.

She glanced at the name, Dave Martin. Then she read the entire report. When she was finished she put the paper down, and faced Jack. "It's hard to believe that someone so healthy can die so suddenly."

"I know what you mean. It doesn't seem fair. But what do you make of the report?"

"He was hit on the back of the head by a falling branch."

"Did you notice where the blow was?"

"The base of the skull?"

"How did the branch hit the base of the skull? Can you tell me that?"

Katie thought about it for several minutes. The ticking of the wall clock echoed ominously in the quiet room. Tick, tick, tick crawled the minutes of their lives. "He was bent over to keep the rain from his face," she said finally. "If you recall, there was a terrible storm that night."

Although she tried to convince herself that it happened that way, somewhere deep inside her, she didn't believe it. Dave would have had to be walking with his chin tucked into his chest. That would cause an awful strain on his neck, never mind making it almost impossible to see where he was going. Maybe she should have asked him what happened when he was standing in her bedroom, but as usual, she didn't think of anything that sensible at the time.

"Let's see the police report," she finally said.

"No can do. Case is still open. They haven't given it to me to file yet."

"How'd you get these?" she asked, curiously.

"Can't tell you that. If I told you I'd have to kill you," he teased. "Besides, if my uncle ever found out I'd used my key to the file room, he'd take it away."

Katie laughed. Then more seriously, she continued. "You don't believe Dave had an accident, do you?"

"Do you?" Jack countered.

"In view of this report, I don't see how. If I was a police officer and I was handed this report, I'd suspect someone killed him."

"Okay, Sherlock, let's hear your version."

"It's a dark, stormy night, my dear Watson. Our poor, unsuspecting victim—that's Dave—is making his way through the woods to meet his mystery date."

"Wait a minute," Jack interrupted. "What mystery date?"

"The person Dave was going to meet."

"How do you know he was going to meet anyone?"

"The night of the storm Dad was driving everyone home. Dave wouldn't wait for him because he said he had to go somewhere before he went home."

"Did he say where?"

"No."

"Do the police know this?"

"I'm sure I told Officer Black. I know I told Dad."

"Okay. Sorry for interrupting. Continue."

"So, Dave is making his way through the woods, his head down against the storm. He doesn't notice that someone is hiding, waiting for him. He goes past the tree where the guy's hiding, and—Whammo! The guy steps out behind Dave, and smacks him with the branch. He's shorter than Dave is and when he swings the branch up it connects with the base of his skull. If the branch struck Dave from the tree, it would have connected closer to the top of the head. Don't you think?"

"Sounds good to me, Sherlock. But how do you know it's a guy?"

"Okay, girl then. There's only one thing that doesn't work."

"And that is?"

"The branch. Wouldn't you be able to tell if the branch was hit by lightning?"

"Good question. Let's just say, for argument sake, that it was. And that the killer picked it up off the ground, after the lightning hit it, and used it to kill Dave."

"Okay," Katie agreed. "Now here's the important question. Can you get finger prints from a tree branch?"

"I believe so. I never have personally, mind you. But I'm sure there must be a way."

"Where is the branch now? I remember seeing them bring it into the police station the day Dad and I were there. Did they find any prints?"

"I don't know."

"How can't you know? Don't you work in forensics? Isn't that where they take prints?"

"I'm studying forensics," Jack told her. "I'm working in the file room at the police station to help pay for school."

"I'm sorry." Katie's cheeks burned. "I thought you were working in forensics." Quickly she changed the subject. "So we have Rick and Dave taken care of. Do you want another soda before we start on Shaun?"

When Katie returned to the table with the sodas, Jack asked. "I've got the autopsy and forensic reports for Shaun. Are you sure you want to see them?"

A small knot began in the pit of her stomach. A sense of foreboding, more profound than anything she'd ever felt, enveloped her. What was it that Jack didn't want her to see? The more important question, did she want to see it? Swallowing, she said, "Let's have them."

Jack handed her the autopsy report first. It began the same as the others: date, sex, age, doctor. She skipped to the more detailed information.

Bile made her throat ache when she read the description of the body. She didn't need pictures to see his bloated, white face. She had her own, indelibly etched on her subconscious. It floated to the surface now, like a bad dream. She forced herself to continue reading.

> ... two small bruises between the base of the skull and the top vertebrae of the neck ... relative to the size and shape of thumb imprints ... placed three-quarters of an inch apart ... two red marks circling the right ankle an eighth of an inch wide ... water in lungs ... cause of death asphyxiation ...

"It wasn't an accident," Katie said simply.

"Doesn't look that way."

"Somebody tripped him with the rope, and then held him down until his lungs filled with water, and he couldn't breathe anymore. He must have been kicking his feet, and that is how he got tangled in the rope." Katie covered her face with her hands, and shuddered. "I can't imagine anything more horrible."

"Neither can I. But it's proof that's needed."

Suddenly Katie found it almost impossible to squeeze fresh air into her burning, desolate lungs. The room was closing in on her. This must have been how Shaun felt. Struggling desperately for air. She fought the nightmare, determined to return to some semblance of normalcy. "Do they have any evidence?" she whispered.

Silently, Jack handed her the other page. The words swam before her eyes.

Forensics Report

Felicity Falls Police Department

... single strand ... human hair ... brown ... female ... between ages ten and twenty ... back of ...

Signed and sealed this 6th day of July ...

Katie dropped the page as if it were on fire. She turned toward Jack. Her eyes showed clearly how stunned she was. "I have brown hair."

Twenty

A MILLION STARS watched the young girl from their stations in the heavens. She inhaled deeply, enjoying the cool, fresh air with its intoxicating pine scent. Ignoring the deck chair, she moved deeper into the shadows, and sat on the floor with her back safely against the wall. Her eyes scanned the surrounding woods, her ears alert to the slightest sound. Somewhere out there was a killer, and she was determined not to be its next victim.

Katie inhaled deeply, keeping the cool night air in her lungs as long as possible before gently exhaling. With each breath, she grew calmer. More relaxed. The tranquil darkness surrounded her, engulfing her with its cool embrace. She welcomed the respite from the jumble of words and images tormenting her fevered brain. Even after looking at all the evidence, and going over repeatedly everything that had happened, she could come to no conclusion, other than the obvious one—she was guilty. She had the beginnings of a miserable headache. There had to be something she was missing. Something so obvious she completely overlooked it.

She would figure it out. *Where were the spooks when you needed them?* With sudden clarity, she knew what she needed to do. *If you want me to help you, then help me,* she thought as loud as she could. *Show me the truth. Who is responsible for doing this to you?*

There was no answer, but that didn't really surprise Katie. In her experience, ghosts only showed up when they felt like it. It didn't matter where she was, or what she was doing, they kept their own schedules. Not that Katie had ever actually tried to summon a spirit. For the most part, she tried to get rid of them. If there were the slightest possibility that Marc was still alive, and deep in her bones Katie felt that he was, then she would summon the ghost of Attila the Hun if possible.

Katie chose a big, old, pine tree near the edge of the porch, and focused on it. Soon all the other trees began to grow fainter, eventually disappearing from her consciousness. There was only her and the big, old, pine tree. Her breathing slowed until it was almost imperceptible. She became one with the night.

A bat flew past the moon, and dined on an unfortunate mosquito. Crickets serenaded the stars. The maniacal laugh of a lone loon echoed across the water. Katie saw these things, not with just her eyes or her ears, but with every molecule of her being.

She knew the exact moment that the clouds covered the moon, leaving the stars to guide the nocturnal hunters on their quests. When the wind picked up she listened for any sound it might carry. She was searching, waiting for a sign that would tell her Marc's whereabouts.

When the shadow moved across her line of vision, she nearly missed it. She was instantly alert. Somebody was skulking through the woods. Katie moved only slightly, to get a better view. There was something strangely familiar about the slender form moving stealthily between the trees.

The figure was barely discernible among the shadows, cloaked as it was in dark jeans and a hooded jacket. Without pausing to consider the consequences of her actions Katie slipped down the stairs, and began to follow the apparition, after all she had asked them to show her the way.

The darkness made it difficult to follow the ghostly figure, by the same token the darkness helped to cover her progress. She held her breath, and counted fully to ten when a twig she stepped on snapped. To her it sounded like an atomic blast, but the figure in front of her didn't even slow down.

Katie hoped she wasn't about to get herself completely lost as she followed the zigzag path of her quarry. Katie lost sight of the shadowy figure several times, only to catch a glimpse of it a few yards ahead.

Not this time.

This time she was sure she had lost it. She was at the spot where she had last seen the figure, but there was still no sign of it. She continued to push through the woods, eyes furtively scanning the area ahead of her. The woods surrounding her had suddenly become very ominous, with predators lurking behind every tree. When she came upon a small thicket she pushed her way through, certain this was the way her shadowy guide had taken. She found herself teetering on the water's edge.

She stood teetering on the shoreline for several seconds before regaining her balance. *Great*, she thought. *Now what?*

The moon broke from behind the clouds, and the light illuminated a figure about a hundred yards down the beach. Katie turned and followed.

This part of the shore was unfamiliar, and she stumbled over rocks and driftwood that littered the beach. The further they travelled the narrower the shoreline became, until she had to scramble through underbrush or walk in the water. The land was much steeper here. There was nowhere for Katie to go, except back the way she came. If the figure in front of her turned around there was no way they wouldn't spot her.

Ahead of her, the shadowy form disappeared once more.

Katie approached the area cautiously, watching for any sign of the shadowed figure, and discovered a small wooden door stuck in the side of the hill.

Katie knew she was looking at an old icehouse. She had seen them before. In pictures, and once when she had gone on a boating trip with her stepfather, Luke. She had pointed to the small door stuck in the side of a hill by the water's edge, and laughed. "What a funny place to build a house," she said.

That was when Luke taught her all about icehouses. They usually dug them into the ground, or the side of a hill along the water's edge. The earth and the heavy wooden doors acted like modern insulation, keeping the cold in, and the heat out. During the winter, the men would chop huge blocks of ice from the frozen lakes and rivers, and store them in the icehouse covered in sawdust. Then during the hot summer months, when it was needed the most, there was ice. Nowadays with everybody owning a fridge or a freezer there was no longer any need for icehouses.

Luke was good like that. Whenever Katie showed an interest in something, he would teach her everything he knew.

Katie put her ear against the heavy door, and listened. She could hear mumbling, but couldn't make out the words. When she heard footsteps approaching on the other side, she stumbling backwards quickly searching for a place to hide. She knew she'd never make it up the hill. It was too steep and densely wooded. If she tried to make her way back along the beach she would be out in the open with no place to hide. The lake effectively blocked her retreat in that direction.

There was only one alternative. She quickly squeezed herself into a copse of cedar bushes beside the small path, and watched the door. The infestation of mosquitoes and other biting insects soon had Katie regretting her choice of hiding places. Waving the pests away only seemed to agitate them more, and after several frustrating attempts to discourage them, she resigned herself to being the main course.

Katie breathed deeply, and forced herself to relax. As her mind cleared, she became more aware of her surroundings. The fragrant cedar, the gently lapping waves, the melodious buzzing of a thousand insects. She listened to the movements inside the icehouse, the clatter of dishes, and the gentle murmur of voices. The voice tugged relentlessly at the edges of her memory, but the harder she tried, the deeper the memory buried itself.

Just when she had decided it was safe to move from her hiding place, the door suddenly opened.

A figure stepped out of the dark icehouse into the bright moonlight. Katie's heart skipped in fear, and anticipation. She stared into the palest blue eyes she'd ever seen. She knew those eyes.

Daina.

They stood staring at each other for a full five count. Without acknowledging her Daina turned, and pulled the heavy door shut behind her. Then she calmly walked past Katie's hiding place without even a glance in her direction, her long brown hair curling on the collar of her pale blue sweater.

Katie waited, scarcely daring to breathe. Ever so slowly, she counted to one hundred. Then she counted to fifty. Finally, after what seemed like an eternity, she was certain that Daina was far enough away she wouldn't see her even if she did look back. Katie left her hiding spot.

With the full moon at her back, Katie approached the door with extreme caution. Slowly she pushed it open.

Twenty-one

A BLAST OF cool air hit her the moment she entered the dark icehouse. It was like opening the fridge door on a hot August afternoon, several degrees cooler than the outside air. Katie shivered, and held the door. She didn't want it swinging shut behind her.

It took several moments for her eyes to adjust enough to see the back wall. Even then, she couldn't penetrate the rest of the darkness. Something scrabbled along the dirt floor in the corner, and Katie cringed. She hated rodents. She clamped her teeth shut, determined not to turn back now. As the moonlight began to filter through the murky interior, she let her eyes wander.

The floor was dirt, packed hard by years of use. Many of the timbers used to shore up the walls now lay useless on the floor. Little piles of dirt strewn around were evidence of the missing boards. A groan, or creak, came from somewhere deeper into the room. Katie tried to peer into the darkness. She inched forward to get a better look. The door creaked behind her. Quickly she caught the door to keep it from slamming shut. It wasn't much, but it was the only source of light she had. Besides she didn't want to get locked in.

Propping the door with her foot to keep it from closing, Katie managed to drag one of the nearest fallen timbers close enough to use as a prop. After satisfying herself that it was secure, she left the relative safety of the open doorway, and moved further into the interior.

Katie was sweating now, despite the cool dampness of the room. She inched her way across the open space to the back wall, careful not to trip over any of the fallen timbers. She allowed her eyes to adjust to the gloom with each step. After what seemed like hours, she finally reached her destination.

She heard another groan, but try as she might, she couldn't make out anything in this murk. She closed her eyes, and counted slowly to ten. It didn't help. When she opened them, instead of adjusting to darkness, she found herself blinded by a light coming from the door.

Hurry, urged the voice inside her head. *Don't get caught.*

Katie took two steps toward the open doorway before stopping herself. *I can't go,* she thought. *Not without making sure that Marc is not here.*

Go. Now. The voice inside her head was frantic, but Katie forced herself to ignore it.

Marc was here. She knew it as surely as she knew her own name. He was here, he was hurt, and she was not going to leave without him.

You know this because. She heard him groan. Was it Marc she heard? It could have been roof timbers groaning under the weight of the earth. Old, rotten roof timbers ready to give way, and drop a ton of dirt on her head.

Stop it. Katie covered her ears with her hands in a futile attempt to stop her own thoughts from driving her mad. Relax, she told herself. Relax and listen.

She closed her eyes. Only this time she listened to everything around her. Her own heartbeat sounded like a tom-tom beating the rhythm of her life. A couple of mosquitoes that had found their way into the icehouse were buzzing seriously close to her ear. A scraping sound to the right of her was probably a rat trying to dig its way through rotted timber.

It took several moments before she was able to distinguish the grating breath from the gentle rippling of the waves outside. It was low and shallow, but definitely breathing. Keeping her left hand on the wall, she slowly maneuvered her way toward the sound.

The room in front of her opened up with each step she took. While behind her, the darkness closed in like a curtain. She had taken about twenty steps when she saw him.

He was slumped against a timber that had pulled partly away from the wall; his arms and legs bound with rope. His eyes closed, his complexion chalky, and dried blood streaked his face from a wound to his brow. His chest barely moved. His breathing was forced and shallow. He was alive, and that was all that mattered.

"Marc." She knelt beside him, and gently pulled his hair back from the laceration. Then wished she hadn't when a fresh trail of blood trickled across his eyelid. She placed her cool hand against his feverish cheek. He was so pale.

"Marc," she whispered. "Wake up." His moan echoed in the silent room, but he didn't open his eyes.

"You need help," she told him. She wasn't sure if it was true, but she had read that a person in a coma could hear when you talked to them. Marc might not be in a coma—but he was unconscious, and if he could hear, she wanted him to know that he wasn't alone.

She struggled to undo the ropes that bound him, all the while keeping up a steady stream of chatter. "I don't know how you got here, Marc. I promise I'll get you out. From the sound of your breathing, the sooner I do the better. Damn." She popped her finger in her mouth, and sucked where she had torn her nail on the rope. After shaking the sting out of it she went back to work on the ropes.

"Sorry about that. I tore my nail just about off. Finally." The knot came undone and she unwound the rope from his wrists. Then taking first one, then the other, she chafed them, trying to jump-start his circulation.

"I'll get your feet now," she said after a few moments. "After all, we can't very well walk out of here with your feet all in knots." His feet were much easier to free than his hands had been. "All done. We can leave now." Katie gently shook Marc's shoulder. "Come on, Marc. You have to wake up now," she pleaded. When there was no visible reaction, she shook him harder. "Wake up, Marc." She raised her voice slightly, and was rewarded with a low moan.

"What am I supposed to do?" she wondered out loud. "I can't carry you. I can't very well leave you here. What if I left you here and Daina came back. What then?" She shook him harder.

She saw his eyelids flutter, right before a shadow moved across the moon immersing them in almost complete darkness. "That's it, Marc," she encouraged him. "Open your eyes. It's me, Katie. We have to get out of here before Daina comes back."

"Too late."

Katie spun around to find Daina standing in the doorway. She was the shadow blocking the moon. "Daina!"

"I don't know why you're so surprised," Daina said calmly. "You know I can't let you take Marc too."

Slowly Katie stood, and faced Daina. Maybe she could bluff her way out. "Am I ever glad to see you, Daina. Look. I've found Marc. He's hurt. Help me get him out of here."

Daina shook her head disdainfully. "Do you really take me for a fool?" She stepped forward and kicked the timber away. "Enjoy your stay," she said scathingly, and pulled the door closed.

"No!" Katie ran as the door slammed shut behind Daina. She yanked on the handle, but it wouldn't budge. Daina must have jammed it with something on the other side. "Open this door," she demanded.

Katie pounded on the steadfast timbers until her hands ached. "Open this door," she sobbed.

Twenty-two

KATIE COULD HAVE sat on the floor, and bawled. How had this happened? Her dad, and Jack, believed her safely locked in the cabin. She was locked in all right. Just not where they thought she was.

Self-pity wasn't going to get her anywhere. Katie pulled herself together, and listened for the sound of Marc's breathing. First, she would do what she could to help Marc. Then, perhaps, the two of them together could figure some way out of this mess.

"Oomph." She found herself sprawled across his legs. Before she could disentangle herself, Marc kneed her in the gut. "Watch it," she complained. She rolled off his legs, and sat up clutching her stomach. His legs kicked out a couple more times before growing still.

"Marc?" she queried tentatively. "Are you awake?" He grunted in answer, and she crawled over to him. Gently she felt for his shoulder, squealing when his hand snaked out, and grabbed her wrist.

"Let go, Marc. You're hurting me." When his grip tightened, she began to panic. "Marc," she spoke sharply. "Let me go."

He loosened his grip but never released her. Katie quit fighting him. She sat back on her haunches, and leaned against him for support. "Marc." She spoke quietly. Calmly. "It's me, Katie. Do you know who I am?" He grunted. She took that for a yes. "Good." She made herself as comfortable as possible, and settled down to wait.

Rubbing her neck, Katie sat up and tried to see in the gloom. It was no use. "Are you awake, Marc?"

"Yeah," he croaked. He didn't sound so good.

Her own throat was scratchy. His must be like the Sahara. She dug into her pocket, and pulled out a pack of gum. Opening a stick, she felt around, and placed it in Marc's hand. "Here," she told him. "Chew on this. It's not lemonade, but it's guaranteed to make spit." Marc's laugh came out a dry cough.

Katie opened her own stick of gum. She chewed until saliva filled her mouth, and swallowed. They needed light. "Do you smoke, Marc?"

"No." His voice sounded slightly better. "Do you?"

"No. Right now, I wish I did. We need some light."

She could hear Marc fumbling around. The small beam of a penlight shining directly into her eyes blinded her. "Oops, sorry," Marc said, and quickly changed the direction of the beam. He handed Katie the light.

Katie splayed the beam around the small room. Maybe she could find something that Daina left behind. Something they could use.

No such luck. She turned off the light to save the battery. "You wouldn't happen to have a penknife in your pocket?" she asked hopefully.

"Sorry."

"Don't worry about it. It was probably a stupid idea anyway."

Sometime later Katie stood up, and stretched. The cold, damp floor was making her legs ache. She could tell by his slow, steady breathing, that Marc was asleep again. As quietly as she could, she made her way across the room using the light only occasionally to mark her progress. Once there, she used the light to study the heavy door. There didn't seem to be any cracks or other damage.

Turning off the light, she again scanned the surface of the door, only this time she was looking for any sign of light shining through from the outside. There was absolutely nothing. It could have been because the moon was behind clouds, but somehow Katie doubted that. It was up there all right, laughing down on her.

Katie found a small piece of wood and tried digging through the cracks in the boards—to no avail. The walls might be crumbling down around them, but they built that door to last.

A fit of coughing disrupted the silence. Katie hurried back to Marc's side. She helped him sit up until the spasm subsided. The heat from his fevered skin seeped through his shirt to brand her fingers. He was shivering, and his chattering teeth were deafening in the silence. Katie was worried. Marc could be seriously ill.

"Do you think you can stand, Marc?" she asked. Maybe it would help if he could get his blood circulating. When Daina comes back, I'll distract her while you get out.

Marc started to protest, and then nodded, but when Katie tried to help him stand, he cried out, and fell back against the wall. "My legs. My legs," he kept saying.

"Sh. It's okay, Marc," she spoke soothingly. "Maybe it'll help if I massage them." Her mother used to rub Katie's legs when she sat cross-legged too long and they fell asleep.

She hadn't been rubbing very long when Marc begged her to stop. It was no use. The shape Marc was in, he wasn't going to be any help to Katie at all. She wasn't even sure that if push came to shove, he would be able to get himself out of the icehouse. Moreover, if Katie had to keep Daina distracted, she wasn't going to be able to help Marc. She would have to come up with a better plan.

Katie made Marc as comfortable as she possibly could. She wrapped her own sweater around him, and then sat against the wall to wait. She was going to need her strength when Daina returned.

The door burst open, and sunlight bathed the small room. It filled every nook and cranny, and enveloped Katie in its warm embrace, even as she squinted against its glare. A dark shadow moved to the centre of the doorway. Panic began as a small ball in the pit of her stomach, only to evaporate when the shadow stepped forward.

Jack.

Katie practically threw herself into his arms. "What took you so long?" she reprimanded. "I didn't think you were ever going to get here."

Jack held her at arm's length. His dark eyes blazed with anger. "Where have you been, Katie?" he demanded. "You were supposed to be in the cabin."

Katie's eyes flew open, effectively vanishing Jack from the icehouse, as Marc cried out in agony. Katie reached for his feverish hand, and squeezed it reassuringly. "Shush," she placated. "Its okay, Marc. Everything will be okay." She hoped her voice sounded more convincing to his ears than it did to hers.

Marc muttered incoherently. Katie smoothed his hair back from his forehead the same way she did for Matthew when he was hurt or ill. It wasn't much, but soon he began to relax under her gentle touch.

"So you and Jack are best friends," she said. It didn't really matter what she said. She felt the need to hear a human voice, even if it was her own. "You're lucky. He's a great guy. A terrific friend. You know, he's been doing everything he possibly can to find you. Everyone is. In fact, just tonight Jack stole copies of reports from the police files. We thought it might help find you, if we could figure out what was going on. Okay. So maybe steal isn't the best word," she mused.

"You're right. Borrowed is a much better word. Did you know Jack was working at the police station to help pay for medical school? Of course you did. You are, after all, his best friend. Do you live in St. Catharines too? ..."

Katie continued talking until Marc sank into a fitful sleep, and then she used the penlight to check her watch. Ten o'clock. That was impossible. It was after eleven when Jack left the cabin. She stared at the minute hand, and counted to one hundred. It didn't move. Great, she forgot to wind it. Again.

She should have let Luke buy her that battery watch for her birthday like he wanted, but this watch had belonged to Grandma Davis. It was Katie's only memento of her late grandmother, and she treasured it dearly. It didn't really matter what time it was. She knew it would be morning soon.

She sat on the cold, damp floor, and thought about her dad. He was going to be so angry when he returned to find her gone from the cabin. She could see it with the clarity of hindsight.

He would unlock the front door and enter the cabin as quietly as possible. Whether it was late tonight, or early tomorrow morning, he wouldn't want to wake her. He'd kick off his shoes, walk silently into the living room, and drop his brief case on the coffee table. Then he would stand and listen, wondering what was different. A cool breeze would tickle the hair on his arms. That's when he'd notice the sliding door open a crack.

He would slide the door open further, and step out onto the deck, expecting to find Katie there getting a breath of fresh air. Instead, he would find an empty deck. Fear would clutch his chest in its icy grip, and he'd run down the hall to her room, throw open the door, and burst in unannounced. Instead of Katie complaining because he didn't knock, silence would greet him.

Fear would turn to anger, because she had defied him. She had left the safety of the cabin to call Jack, and then again to follow a shadow. His anger at her would turn to anger at whoever was responsible for her disappearance. He would alert the police, and when they couldn't find her, he would have to call Luke and Mom.

Katie couldn't imagine anything worse than being told your child was missing. Viciously, she swiped at a stray tear.

This was her fault. She had to find a way to get herself and Marc out of here.

When the door was finally opened, it was still dark. Katie blinked several times, and then squinted against the glare of the flashlight. Daina played the beam of light over Marc's prone body. "Hi, Marc," she said cheerfully, as if they had just run into each other on the beach. She didn't even seem to notice when Marc didn't answer. She kept on talking. "I've brought you something to eat. You must be getting hungry," she said as she hung the flashlight on a nail in the wall.

As Katie watched, Daina placed her pack on the floor beside Marc, and pulled out a small packet. "I made ham," Daina said. "I wasn't sure if you liked mustard or mayonnaise, so I used both." Daina unwrapped the sandwich with the same care one would use with a precious present. Then she leaned over Marc, and stuck the sandwich against his dry lips.

"There you go, Marc. Take a nice big bite." Marc's breathing was coming in shallow, grating breaths, and he never moved.

"He can't eat, Daina," Katie tried to tell her. "He needs a doctor."

Daina didn't acknowledge Katie in any way. She just kept talking to Marc, and trying to get him to eat the sandwich. Katie wasn't even sure if Daina realized she was there.

If only she could make her way to the door without drawing Daina's notice. She could run back to the campground and bring help. She lifted herself up on her hands and her heels and sidled a couple of inches. Daina paid her no mind. Katie scuttled like a crab until she was behind Daina. Then she flipped herself over, and began to crawl toward the door. She listened to Daina talking to Marc, and watched the distance between her and the door diminish.

Six feet...four...two.

Marc groaned. He was beginning to come around. He brushed at the sandwich tickling his lips, causing Daina to drop it.

"Look what you did," she screamed, startling Katie.

Katie turned her head to see what was going on, and bumped into the door. Daina jerked around at the noise, and glared at Katie. There was no longer any doubt in her mind. Daina knew she was there.

"Where do you think you're going?" Daina spat out.

"Home." Katie jumped up and jerked the door open. She threw herself through the opening, and started to run. She could feel Daina's breath on her neck.

Twenty-three

THE MOON WAS playing hide and seek with the clouds, and it was while the moon was hiding that Katie tripped over a piece of driftwood. She threw her arms out to break her fall. Before she could right herself, Daina fell on her like a wild cat clawing and scratching, and pulling Katie's hair. Katie rolled over and knocked Daina to the ground. She didn't wait to see if Daina was all right before getting to her feet, and running full out.

Her heart pounding in her ears drowned out the sound of pursuit. Katie felt the hands at her back. In that instant, she found herself spitting beach out of her mouth. She had to admit that she could not escape Daina. Even if she made it along the shore, there was still the hill to climb, and Daina knew this area a lot better than Katie did. She could work her way through the woods and be waiting for Katie.

Furiously, Katie rolled over. Kicking out she knocked Daina off her feet. Then half rising, she hurdled herself at the fallen girl. Arms and legs tangled as they rolled around in the sand, each one vying for the top position. Exhaustion, finally took its toll on Katie, and she found herself on the bottom.

With a wild look in her eye, Daina sat on Katie's chest, pinning her arms to her sides with her legs. Katie's struggles were futile. Daina kept her pinned to the ground.

Katie thought about shouting for help, and then decided to save her breath. From what she'd seen of this part of the beach there weren't any homes nearby. If she got her arms free she'd grab one of the chunks of driftwood that littered the beach, and brain Daina.

Katie's vision began to clear, and her eyes widened in horror. Daina was perched above her with a large chunk of the coveted driftwood raised over her head. Katie screamed as the makeshift weapon came down with sickening accuracy. She managed to turn her head at the last moment, and avoid the full impact of the blow.

Her scalp itched like crazy. With every fiber of her being, she longed to scratch it. Her arms lay heavy at her sides, and she was unable to raise them. Blood oozed from the gash on her temple. Like an army of ants crawling over a rotting peach, it trickled through the matted strands of her hair, down her cheek, and into her ear. The coppery smell filled her nostrils making her feel faint.

With a sick feeling, she watched helplessly as Daina again raised the stump over her head. She wouldn't survive another blow.

"Daina."

The voice was like a catalyst. Daina froze—arm raised above her head. Instinct took over. Katie arched her back. Daina's balance was precarious, and she began to teeter.

Katie heard the low warning growl, and terror held her frozen. The dog was a young, strong German Shepherd with large, sharp teeth that glistened in the moonlight. It leapt effortlessly over Katie's head towards Daina. Its front paws caught her full in the chest toppling her to the ground.

Daina's scream of terror matched Katie's own, until the darkness engulfed her.

She was wandering through a void. There was no sight, no feeling, and no sound—except the irritating buzz of a lone bee, or was it a hungry mosquito. The harder she tried to block out the irritating buzzing the louder it grew, until it turned into the familiar hum of voices. One voice in particular stood out.

Daina.

She was talking to someone. Who? Katie closed her eyes against the distraction created by her inky surroundings, and concentrated on Marc. Slowly the shadows parted, like the curtain on the opening scene.

Several strangers gathered around Marc. Some wore police uniforms, while others were in plain clothes. One man, she knew he was a doctor because he was wearing a white lab coat and a stethoscope, checked Marc's pulse, and then shone a small penlight into his eyes. Katie flinched against the glare, but Marc just lay there, completely unaware of what was going on around him. When the man was finished his brief

Final Justice

examination they moved Marc onto a flat board, and secured
the harness.

Katie scoured every corner of the room. Daina wasn't
there.

When she opened her eyes, the curtain of darkness fell
once again, expunging Marc and the others from her view. A
cool breeze caressed her hot flesh, and she shivered almost
imperceptibly. Daina's voice was louder now. Katie could
discern what she was saying and she was shocked.

"I know. I couldn't believe it myself. When I saw her
sneaking down the path something told me to follow her, and
so I did. Then I saw her go into the icehouse. I know I should
have gone to tell someone. What was I going to tell them? That
I saw Katie making lone, nocturnal visits to an icehouse that I
didn't even know she knew about. There's no law against that.
I had to find out what she was doing.

"So I hid in the bushes and waited until she came out.
When I thought she was safely up the path I started to go in.
She must have seen me hiding and just pretended to leave,
because when I started into the icehouse she snuck up behind
me, and shoved me in. That's when I found Marc, and I
realized she'd locked him in there. I tried but I couldn't find a
way out. It seemed like I was in that dark place forever, but
she finally came back. When she was busy with Marc, I tried to

crawl away, but she must have heard me because she suddenly came after me. She was so angry. I was afraid of what she would do. I ran. I know I shouldn't have left Marc alone with her, but I was afraid. I tried to get away but she just kept coming after me. When she knocked me to the ground, I knew I had to defend myself. You would have done the same?" she whined when they didn't react the way she wanted. "She'd already killed Shaun and Dave. There was no reason to think she wouldn't kill me too."

Katie closed her eyes, and breathed deeply of pine and old spice. The beach was ablaze with the brilliance of a dozen lanterns. She knew she was lying on the same type of board as Marc, her arms and legs securely fastened. While she watched helplessly, two men lifted the board. It tipped slightly, and Katie dug her fingernails into the sides in a desperate attempt to keep from falling. It didn't occur to her that the straps would not let her fall.

"Be careful." Her father sounded angry. It was funny how she could hear him so clearly, but his image wouldn't come to mind.

Daina was still trying to convince the officer that she was innocent when he pulled out a pair of handcuffs. Katie almost laughed aloud at the astonished look on Daina's face. In the next heartbeat, Daina turned, and ran—straight into Jack's arms. As Katie watched in silence, the police cuffed her, and led her down the beach.

Jack said something. She saw his lips move but couldn't make out what he was saying. Then with a short, sharp whistle he turned, and followed Daina and the officer along the beach. Katie's heart leapt to her throat when a German Shepherd appeared from the bushes, and snapping at his heels followed Jack.

They were placing Katie on the deck of a pontoon boat when the board tipped suddenly. Katie cried out in panic. Her eyes flew open, only to close quickly against the glare of a dozen lanterns. Once settled on the boat, she allowed herself to relax. The gentle roll of the waves and the steady rhythm of Marc's breathing alongside her, helped lull her into a fitful sleep.

Twenty-four

KATIE FLICKED OFF the TV, and inwardly fumed. "Where are they?" she muttered aloud. She'd been waiting impatiently for over an hour, ever since the doctor had finished examining her.

She thought back to the doctor's visit. Doctor Campbell was a nice man. A little on the plump side, with completely white hair, ruddy cheeks, and smiling blue eyes, he reminded her of a dwarf. However, his hands were steady and his voice was strong, belying his appearance of frailty.

The doctor gave her a clean bill of health. "A little dehydrated, and a slight concussion. Nothing that a lot of fluids and a couple of days rest won't cure," he had declared with a wink.

"Great. So when can I go home?"

"I want to keep you under observation. Just overnight," he had added quickly when he saw her look of consternation. "I'm sure you will be able to go home first thing in the morning."

One night won't be too bad, she thought. "I don't have to stay in this bed, do I?" she asked. "I mean, I can go visit Marc, can't I?"

"Marc?"

Doc looked puzzled. "Marc, my friend," she asked, fear knotting her stomach. When he didn't answer immediately, she hurried to explain. "The boy who was brought in with me last night." Confusion mingled with fear. Had she only imagined that Marc was safe? Was he still missing?

"Oh, yes," understanding dawned in the doctors blue eyes. "The young man with the head wound."

"He's all right isn't he?" The beginnings of panic made her words terse. What wasn't the doctor telling her?

"The young man isn't with us anymore." The room began to sway, and tears formed in Katie's eyes, before the doctor hurried on. "He was flown to Toronto early this morning. His wounds were far too serious for us to treat here." He seemed to consider what he should say before he continued. "He has a serious skull fracture, and there was some swelling of brain tissue. That, combined with his high fever, made it imperative that we move him to the larger hospital. They have the facilities to treat him there."

"But he is going to be okay, right?" Katie asked hesitantly.

"I can't guarantee anything. We just have to wait, and hope he wakes up soon."

Katie snapped on the TV again, and began flicking through the three stations that came in clearly. One was the old black and white Alfred Hitchcock movie she'd turned off earlier. One was a basketball game, which she would normally have chosen. Today she opted for the third choice. The local news.

"Missing teenager, Marc Randall, was flown to Sunnybrook Hospital early this morning where he is being

treated for dehydration and head trauma. The police do have a suspect in custody, but are not releasing further information at this time. We will keep you informed ..."

Katie flicked off the television when her father walked through the door. "It's about time," she complained. "Where have you been? What have you found out about Marc? Doc said his brain is swelling." She returned her father's hug, brushing off his inquiries as to her own state of health. "I'm fine. Doc says I need to rest for a day, and drink plenty of fluids. Before you say anything, I've already had four things of juice, a jug of water, some rubbery, green jelly stuff for breakfast, and when I complained that I was going to starve if they didn't give me something solid to eat, they gave me some watery old tapioca pudding." She rolled her eyes in disgust. "Forget about me. How's Marc?"

Her dad pulled a chair closer to the side of the bed, and sat down. "There's some fluid on the brain. They've drained it the best they can but if he doesn't wake up soon they may have to operate." He reached for his daughter's hand, grinning when she returned his squeeze. Never before had he thought it even remotely possible that he wouldn't see her again. If not for her lucky stars, she could have easily ended up in a coma like Marc—or worse.

"Have you called Mom?" Katie asked. She crossed her fingers, and chewed on her bottom lip anxiously.

"I called the ranger station when we couldn't find you."

Katie cringed, inwardly. She was glad she wasn't a party to that conversation. Her mother went ballistic whenever she thought her children might be in danger. "Was she totally crazed?"

"Yes and no," her father hedged.

Katie noticed it immediately. It was something he was always on her case about. "Be concise and honest," he would say. "Don't hedge." She called him on it now. "How can she be crazed, and not crazed, at the same time."

Her dad had the grace to look slightly discomfited. "I told her I just wanted to let her know that I was taking you to the Cayman's for a week."

"Dad!" She'd always wanted to go to the Cayman Islands.

"I didn't see any reason to worry her. You were safe by the time she returned my call."

"How long was I missing?" It had seemed like days. Maybe being in such total darkness made it seem that way.

"A little less than twenty four hours."

"Twenty four hours. And Mom didn't return your call."

"I didn't call until 7 in the morning. I got back just after midnight, and you were gone." His dark brows furled into a scowl. "We'll discuss your disobedience later," he said. "Ted, Officer Black, was with me, and we began the search immediately. When we hadn't found you by sunrise, I knew I had to make the call." Her dad chuckled quietly. "It seems you weren't the only one missing."

"What do you mean?"

"It seems the rangers had quite a time contacting your mother. They got to the campsite at about seven thirty but it was already deserted. Luke had them up and moving before first light. When they finally found them, Luke was happily filming a doe and her fawn, completely unaware that the day had slipped away."

"I'm glad Mom won't have to know what happened," Katie said.

"She'll need to know, Katie."

"But why? I'm all right. I don't have any broken bones to explain away. And my bruises will be completely healed by the time we get back from the Cayman's." Her father raised one eyebrow in a questioning gesture. "We have to go to the Cayman's, Dad. You told Mom we were going. Do you want to be the one to tell her you lied?"

"Point taken. However, Irene is still going to have to know. There may be a trial."

"A trial." Katie was dismayed. She hadn't thought of a trial. She was hoping that it was over. That she wouldn't even have to think about Daina again. "Why'd she do it, Dad? Why did she kill those boys?"

"Daina is a very disturbed young lady. She has been for a long time. When she was five, she smothered her baby brother while he was asleep in his crib. At first, they thought it was SIDS, but the autopsy revealed a feather lodged in his nostril. Considering there was no pillow in his crib, this led to the conclusion that someone had held a pillow over his face until he quit struggling. The ensuing investigation led to Daina spending the next eight years in an institution for the mentally disturbed in British Columbia."

"How do you know all this?"

"The doctor who performed the autopsy on Bobby Mitchell is the forensics expert I met a while back while I was investigating a murder in Michigan, Martin Frasier. He agreed to put in a little overtime for me. Yesterday we sent a hair sample that was found on Shaun's body to Vancouver."

"You mean the brown, female hair, like mine."

"How did you? Never mind. You can tell me all about it later. As I was saying, Martin did a DNA test on the strand of hair. He promised to have the results yesterday. That's why I had to go out. I wanted to be there when he called.

"Anyway, the DNA from the hair matched a sample they had on file; the one taken from Daina ten years ago. That's when Martin told us about the Mitchell case. Ted called the captain, and had an undercover officer assigned to watch Daina. We didn't want to tip our hand and alert her that she was a suspect. We were hoping she would lead us to Marc. After all, why would she think anyone was following her, when they already had the perfect suspect? You."

Bill helped himself to a glass of water, and then waited patiently until Katie drank one before continuing. "You can imagine how I felt when I got back to the cabin and discovered you were missing, after promising me you would be safe. Daina was seen returning to the apartment shortly before we arrived. She was alone, and there was no way of knowing where she had been. I called Jack. He told me that he'd been by earlier." Katie fidgeted beneath her father's disapproving frown. "He also said you promised to lock all the doors as soon as he left, but apparently I'm not the only one you don't listen to. The patio door wasn't only unlocked, it was open."

"I needed some air. It felt like the walls were closing in on me. I was only going to step outside for a moment. Then I saw Daina sneaking through the woods and I didn't think. I just followed," her voice faded away, as a memory flickered briefly. When she followed Daina from the cabin, she was wearing dark jeans and a dark hoody, but when she saw Daina at the icehouse, she was wearing a moss colored sweater, and light blue track pants. Now that she thought about it, there was no reason for Daina to go past the cabin to get to the icehouse. It would have been easier, and quicker, for her to go straight from her home.

Katie swallowed, as a thought occurred to her. Shaun wore dark jeans and a hoody. Did Shaun lead her to Marc? Was that his way of helping his friend before it was too late, and ensuring they caught Daina? The next time she saw Shaun she would ask him, if she saw him again.

"That's obvious. Maybe next time you will stop and think." He smiled to take the sting out of his words. He was too glad she was okay to stay mad at her long.

"But why did Daina kill them?" Katie asked again. She still wasn't sure why.

"I'm not positive. Nobody but Daina knows for sure, and she's not talking. Martin has a theory, and I'm inclined to agree. We know that when she killed her brother it was because she blamed him for taking her parents away from her. She'd been the center of their lives for five years when suddenly, along comes a baby that does nothing but sleep and cry, and her parents adore it. All the attention that was hers is now this interloper's. She wanted to punish her parents for what she perceived as their desertion of her, but they were too big, so she turned her anger on her brother. After all, he was the reason they turned from her. She held the pillow over his tiny little face until he quit all his struggling. What she hadn't expected was that her parents, instead of turning their attention back to her, would send her away."

"Why did they let her out of the hospital? Didn't they think she might hurt someone else?"

"Her doctors said she was cured. That she no longer felt the need to be the center of attention, and she was no longer a threat."

"Well they don't know Daina very well. I've only known her for a little more than a week, and I know she always wants to be the center of attention. She flirts with everyone, and when someone pays attention to anyone else she gets really angry."

Visions of Daina flew threw her mind. Daina glaring with hatred at Shaun, when he accidently threw grass on her.

Daina's barely concealed anger when Dave asked Katie to play ball. Daina flirting shamelessly with Marc. Daina trying to monopolize the conversation the day she had invited Katie to lunch, and then turning nasty when her father included Katie in the conversation.

It was that same day after lunch that Daina talked about Rick. Katie could still hear the pain in her voice. "You shouldn't have left me," she'd said. At the time, Katie thought she was still grieving over Rick's death. Now she realized Daina was angry that Rick was returning to his girlfriend. If he hadn't told Daina about his girlfriend would he be alive now?

What had set her off? Was it because the others had gone out of their way to include Katie—and by doing so had inadvertently excluded Daina? Or, did it go deeper than that?

The door swung open, and Katie jumped. With the thoughts of Daina so vivid in her mind, she almost expected to see Daina walk through the door.

It was Jack. "Marc's awake," he said, with a smile. He didn't look the least bit angry with her. "He's going to be fine. The doctors said if he continues to improve he can come home in about a week."

"That's the best news I've had all day." Katie couldn't help but smile as she drowned in the depth of his dark eyes.

The warm, tropical sun beat down on her as she lay on the deserted, white sand beach. They had only been here three days, and all ready she was as brown as a native was. She credited the hours spent snorkeling in the clear green waters, and the long solitary walks along the shore, for her improved condition. It didn't hurt, either, that Jack had come to the cabin before they left, and told them that there wasn't going to be a trial. Daina would spend the rest of her days in the institution where she was truly happy—the center of attention.

Katie signed her letter with a flourish, and stuffed it in the envelope. With any luck, she might see Jack before he got the letter.

He did promise to visit before school started.

About the Author

LYNN HENDERSON was born in the Haliburton Highlands more than half a century ago. She loves to read and write, and spend time with her grandchildren. She has been married to a wonderful man for over thirty years, has two wonderful children, and two beautiful granddaughters.

She also writes for adults under the name Lynn Marie Simpson.